The Greatest Ace

The Story of a Dog and a Farm

Keith J. Dittrich

NEBRASKA
AGRARIAN PRESS

Contents

To my brother, John, an unsung hero of Rural America.

To Merle, Janette and Allen

Josh, and Claire

And my loving wife, Tammy.

Introduction

Dogs. I'm lucky to be one. Most humans like dogs. I like humans, but they think they're superior to us. That's just silly, though, given our strengths and sensory capabilities - well beyond what humans can do. Sure, they have noses and sure, they have ears. But I've yet to see one get excited, like I do, about the literal thousands of scents I smell while glory riding in the back of a pickup truck, or hear the movement and mutterings of what I hear at night. It would knock them off their feet.

In the dark, they sleep, and don't seem to sense a thing - well, except for my barking, when I talk to another dog howling in the distance. Or maybe I smell a 'critter crossing the road beyond the boundary. I doubt they can do that. Lucky for them I'm on guard.

I should mention my sense of direction, and my instinctual wisdom about dangers, predators, and hunting - and even my faith and loyalty. But then there's my sense of the unknown – of the beyond, and that which is forgotten. Watch me as I gaze into the distance intently, with ears alert and nose twitching, taking it all in. Every life's heartache and joy is reverberating between the stars, just waiting to be felt and remembered. I may be a farm dog but I still come from the wild - with my unrestrained instincts now attuned to human emotions. And I do so love the humans who are my loving domestic masters.

We are all descendants of somebody, something. Yet we are transient too. Some of us are migrants, maybe from another country, or between states... States are always changing. No less, the state of fairness and injustice. There are lots of states to deal with in my story.

Nebraska is where I live and it's the place I love. There're rolling hills of farmland, and valleys with trees and water. I've rode in the pickup over rivers like the Platte, and Loup, and Elkhorn. There's even one called the Snake. I live in the northeast part, on a farm that grows crops, and livestock - and kids! They have always been my best friends!

Strong, willing pioneers settled this region in the late 1800s, building houses of dirt and prairie grass sod, or dug into the side hills to protect them from winters more harsh than you can imagine. There's a site just north of the place here where one was built. It's all gone, and now only a badger lives there. I've dug for that badger, and smelled the remnants of the humans that lived there - rusty iron, an old leather harness, pieces of a broken plate, and a tarnished, bent baby spoon. I bet hard times ensued quickly for most of these settlers, as they worked to build their lives here. They probably didn't have the knowledge to understand this environment. Yet some of them prevailed, and made space and place for the following generations of farm families that I tell the stories of here.

We dogs played an essential role in the development of our Midwestern country. My ancestors have hunted, herded, protected, and provided companionship to the farmers and ranchers who lived here. To this day, that's a fact. It probably would not have happened without us.

Dogs don't speak the same outward language that humans do. Internally they do, though. In the case of a human, words are just thoughts that are spoken. But the thoughts are there in both human and animal, just the same. It's just more of an effort for us to express them, and turn them into something both can understand. I like to use my eyes, mostly. They can say a whole lot.

With that, let me tell you the story of one farm dog. Me.

My Beginnings

I was born into a litter of ten puppies. They were warm to sleep with, and I would cuddle up with them, and bury my nose in the soft pile of their furry bodies. When my mother came into the nest, we would crawl around, following her sound and scent, before our eyes opened. She had a great smell of food and safety, and gave us warm licks. As my eyes began to open, I realized the other pups looked a lot like me, yet I was a different color and had a white chest and belly that the others didn't. I also had a distinct marking just above my white patch. It was shaped like a spade on a card deck. I heard my owners notice it one day, and say "Let's call him Ace". I kinda liked that.

We lived in Oklahoma, in the suburb of some big city. Our parents were top dogs in their breed, with a pedigree better than most, I heard. I'm pretty sure I was the best pup of the litter too. I did notice that my brothers and sisters were growing faster than me. But I was bred to be a small Australian shepherd so little was good, right?

I played with my brothers and sisters a lot. Since I was light, they could pull me around without effort. Sometimes it got kind of rough. Soon, there were fewer and fewer siblings to play with. One at a time, someone would come and pick up a pup, cuddle it, and then leave with it. I missed them for a while but, given there was always another one to play with, it was no big deal. It seemed I was getting roughed up a bit less too.

Then, one day, it was down to two of us. The door opened, and some stranger came in and picked me up. I acted my best and even licked the person's fingers. Sure, I whimpered a little when they put me down. My playmate was next. She squirmed in the person's hands while they held her to their chest. I figured she was excited, and about to pee in their arms, literally messing up the whole thing. But she didn't.

"We'll take her," the lady said.

And suddenly, my last friend was gone. My mother was already moved, having weaned us from her milk. She was still in the house, though. I could smell her and hear her bark once in a while. I missed her nuzzling on my belly, and I sure missed the milk. Now, I was all alone. But I was okay.

I guess they saved the best for last. It was pretty quiet in that nest the ensuing nights and pretty slow the following days. Most of the time, I was waiting for the door to open, and sometimes I chased my tail, just to play with something that moved. I was quick but it still seemed to get away from me.

About eleven o'clock one night, the light came on in my room. I was sleeping, curled up into my own ball. With squinting eyes, I saw a couple of fellows. They chatted with the people of the house, one of whom was holding the door. It seemed like this time the picking was going to be different, since I was the only one left. Kind of like the last apple in the basket - probably the ripest sweetest one. So I thought of myself sort of like that. I sure wished they would have picked a better time to look at me, since I wasn't in my best form at all.

It didn't make much difference, though, I guess, since they just walked in and swept me up out of the bed I had made by going round and round in some shavings. One man tucked me under his arm. They both walked me out of the room and then sat down and filled in some papers. *Papers.* Well, I was about to ready to use the ones in my quarters. But I held it in, and just hunkered down in the guy's lap. The new guys handed over a few green bills to my owners. I had been so excited, waiting to get picked all this time!

Suddenly, I was outside my safe zone, and panting though it wasn't even warm. *Where am I going? Who are these guys? What about mom? Will I ever see her again?* I thought, while squirming a bit.

Thank you, sir, but I think I better get back now, digging in with my claws to jump off his lap.

He let out an "Ouch!" then grabbed me by the scruff of my neck.

This isn't starting out like I had planned, I thought. There was a handshake between the men, as they left the house and walked out to the street. I was left dangling for the moment.

There was a green SUV parked out front, and the rear opened up. I thought they would just set me down in it but instead they opened up a small kennel box and slipped me in. It was smelly plastic and had lots of vent holes, with a mesh front door. I could easily see out, and up in the blue inky sky were some stars flickering strong enough to be seen through the glow of the street lights. *I'm pretty sure I can chew through this door if I need to.*

One thing they had forgotten to do was ask me if I liked riding in the rear, especially turned backwards. But I thought maybe it would be all right. I didn't even whimper when it went dark close to midnight. I was tired so I put my head down between my front paws and peered through a peep hole at the street lights going by, one by one. I started counting them but soon lost track, as my mind wandered back to my nest, and my mother, and my siblings. *Wow,* I wondered, *did my brothers and sisters have this same experience?*

The car I was in headed down the road - north, I'm quite sure, since my mother taught me which was it was. Mostly I was looking south, though, given the position of my crate and the peepholes. Direction is important to a dog. I heard my mother say "Always know which way you're headed." I hoped at least one of the men had been taught that mom lesson too.

Here I was, crammed in between suitcases and luggage and other stuff that goes with going on a trip. I can imagine going on a trip in the woods, and all I would have along is me. And maybe a friend. *Humans must be different when going on a trip. I sure miss my old home right now.*

Soon it became clear that sitting backwards in the night was not for me. I whined and whimpered a bit to get their attention but to no avail. It wasn't long, and things began to happen. Though I felt the need to leave, I couldn't. But my inside stuff didn't feel the same restrictions. There I sat in the mess, in the dark, and on the move in the night to some unknown place. I was used to bad smells, but the men started talking and coughing. *I'm so embarrassed.*

They opened the windows as they sped north on the highway. Fresh air blew through my dog space in the back, and the breeze carried new smells I'd never known. The men stopped at a darkened, closed gas station along the interstate. Both got out, and one came back to get me. I huddled in the back corner, and looked up at them shaking as they shone a flashlight on me. *Here I am in the night with two men on the road, and I'm so sick. Where's mom when you need her most?* When a big hand reached back to me I cowered. *This is it.* One man found a water hose and gave me a quick bath right there. That's the worst bath I think I ever had. *This growing up thing and moving away from home isn't quite what I was thinking.*

They must have seen my distress, and that I was really shaking now.

"Hey, little pup. It's going to be alright," as he reached for a towel in the back and wrapped it all around me. "Let's get you warmed up and dried off. It'll be alright."

He took both his hands and rubbed the towel all around me, doing the best he could to dry me off. Suddenly I was bundled up and being held against the man's chest with both arms, as he walked behind the car. I was reminded of being cuddled up to my mom not too long ago, and my shaking stopped. My heart wasn't beating so fast anymore. I looked out into the night and saw stars all around. All I could hear was the sound of cars going by, and the slower beat of the man's heart against me.

He placed me carefully back into the box, now cleaned-up, and with a new pad. It didn't feel so bad in there now but I was exhausted. We made the long trip through that night into the dawn, I guessed to my new home. I slept for a while until a glimmer of light started coming into the side window.

"We're in Nebraska," one man said to the other.

The sun was getting pretty high when the men stopped at a drive-through in a town, and got some coffee. I could smell the complicated aroma just like I did when I saw my first owners every morning. Soon, we stopped again at a green area, like a park. The big lid opened up on the back of the car. The man picked me up out of my carrier and set me down onto the green grass, in the sun, and breeze, and glory. This was especially good after the long night's ride.

"Here you go," the one man said.

"Hi, Daddy! A new puppy! He's so great!" said a little girl, as she ran up to meet me from across the way. She picked me up, hugging me tight to her chest. I licked her face with all my might. Then we ran in circles and figure eights all around, as she playfully chased me. It was so much fun when I let her catch me. She'd scoop me up into her arms, and rough up my belly hair.

"I can't wait to get you to the farm, to see all the other animals," she told me. "I hope our bigger dog gets along with you. You can sleep out in the barn with them all."

Farm? Big dog? Barn? There must be some mistake. I had been planning on sleeping on the man's bed in the house, and certainly not with another bunch of animals. *And as far as the big dog goes, well, I'm a pretty tough pup so it better get along with me.* Suddenly a shiver went through me, and I put my nose low into the corner of her elbow.

"You'll be able to help protect the farm from all the varmints, and chase the cows with the big dog. Dad said the other dog should have lasted longer, but that's how it goes on the farm."

Lasted longer? Chase cows? From what I've heard, cows are pretty big compared to my size. What happened to the other dog? Wait a minute, I come from the suburbs, and have a pedigree. There must be some mistake here. But she climbed into the vehicle, with me in her arms, and we drove away.

The Old Farm

The story of the place is known to me. There are my own recollections but also memories from those long-gone from here; whispers in the wind; murmurs from the stars....

The barn had already stood for seventy-five years, when they took over the farm amidst the hilly croplands of Nebraska. It was large, traditional, and had been painted a classic red obviously too few times in its life. It had a cupola surrounded by worn-out grayed wood shingles. The weathervane on top had one arm missing, so it only showed west or east. Its foundation was teetering and falling out, leaving large gaps one could see through. Given the history of hard times here, the past owners just couldn't afford to keep it up.

Upon opening the two-piece doors with hook clasps, the hinges creaked. The top section had one hinge missing so it hung at an angle against the siding, and banged in the wind. Inside it had mostly dusty dirt floors, and was quiet. There was a maze of gates, stanchions for milking cows, and feed bunks in stalls for horses or whatever animal needed out of the weather. Rusty baling wire held together broken boards. Old worn leather harnesses hung from nails driven into the huge wooden beams that held the upper hay mow. There was a small feed room with no window so it was dark when peering in. Scattered oat hulls mixed with mouse droppings covered the floors. For them, it was a safe haven from cats - a place where small creatures could find something to eat.

The stairs lead to the hay mow above. The way was walled in, with one turn. One never knew what was around the corner so the final step was taken with trepidation as you went into the huge open room. Likely, an old yellow tomcat would look up in alarm with big glaring eyes, and head low, and then run to his escape route somewhere along the side. A few pigeons would find their way in, and sit and coo on the iron trestle high up in the mow. Rays of light hit the floor through places in the roof where no shingles existed anymore. Straw bales in one corner sat on the bed of old hay with smells of mold, age, and raccoon scat. Water stains on the rafters told the story of rot that had already set into the wooden structure.

Many animals dwelled in the old barn over the years - brown cows and white-faced baby calves, huge draft horses tired from a day's work, chickens that found their way inside, and cats who waited for a rat to emerge from under a plank. I suppose numerous farm dogs like me made their way into the barn, following their masters around while chores were completed or helping them guard a door from a potential animal escape or unwanted entry.

An old handmade milking stool rested by a stanchion. There a cow was held for milking while she ate from the bunk. The chair consisted of a short block of wood with a board seat nailed on top. It was usually a kid's job in the morning and evening to milk her, while teetering on the stool, draining as much as the Guernsey might have. There was always a prayer that a pesky fly would not land on her belly, making her kick the bucket over. When that did happen, the steel pail would clang and pour its contents on the straw covered dirt floor, while the child would stand up in disgust, wondering what Mother would say when the bucket came to the kitchen nearly empty.

Soon after Evan bought the place, the barn was bulldozed down, since it had outlived its use and was beyond repair. It was not a good day, that day.

The farmhouse, only fifty steps from the barn, had fared much better. It sat on a higher bit of ground and was nearly as massive as its red neighbor. Between them stood the silver-colored windmill which pumped water for both humans and livestock. By then it had been converted to electricity, yet the vanes turned in the breeze, with a scratchy, creaking sound coming from the old gearbox above.

The house was painted white. It was three stories high and had so many windows I never tried to count them all. The high concrete porch steps on three sides were crumbling by then and in need of repair. It had wooden shingles, too, with some missing, but not too many as to leak like the barn. The screen doors were rusty and in need of replacement.

I know what it looks like since it is still standing, and I get to lie on the kitchen floor some evenings. Most farm dogs live outside and don't enter the house.... The front porch has two big columns holding up a flat roof above. It doesn't have any railings but has a big front entrance door that leads to a parlor. When I enter that way, I walk through the big rooms, pass a stairway, then head into the dining room before my nose meets the kitchen smells. I figure the second floor is where the bedrooms are but I've never dared go up the stairs. That's where Evan, Ella, Jamie, and Clara slept during my time there, I'm sure, since I've heard them talk to me from upstairs windows at night when I've barked at neighbor dogs or howled at the moon. Dogs must be a little nocturnal, since a good part of protecting the farm comes during the night. Above those windows, are small ones up on the roof-level. They are usually all dark, and I never see anyone there. Those windows kind of bother me.

The day Evan moved to the farm it was overgrown with trees and bushes. There was an old fancy wire mesh fence with big concrete border posts separating the house yard from the farm yard. I suppose the previous owners didn't want pigs and cows tearing up the lawn. To the south were shade trees, including one big cottonwood. Evergreens also stood there and provided color, even during the winter months. All these trees had been planted much later than when the house was built but were mature and in need of pruning, at least. I watch Evan work on the yard now, with a look of pleasure on his face. Many evenings in the summer, he can be seen riding a big mower machine around just before sundown. The sound and the smell of this stay with me and remind me of warm summer days. When he is done, it is always fun to bound around and roll in the pungent-smelling green grass.

A granary sat to the north of the barn and farmhouse. It had been built later than both, around a time things were good on the farm, and there were profits to pay for it. This wooden structure had a wide alleyway with overhead bins from where grain could drop. They were filled by a conveyor elevator that was placed at the side, and from an opening in the roof. On each side of the alleyway were slatted cribs built for ear corn, to let it dry in the air after it had been harvested. This was the perfect place for rodents to habituate, since there was food and endless hiding places between the ears of corn and under the wooden floor.

In later years it was converted to a horse stable, after the barn was demolished. This is how I knew it. It became my hangout, since that's where my food dish was located, and my doghouse sat out in front. Evan and his daughter Clara always ended the day by feeding me, the cats, and the horses before they went into the house for supper. Then I followed and lay down on the front porch with my paws hanging over the edge.

There I would look out at the stars, and the moon rising above the trees. And listen intently.

Flying Aces

Jessie was pulling the one-row cultivator with Jack and Jim as team. They were working the field of corn just west of the farmhouse. Gracie skipped alongside the slow moving rig so she could be close to her father and the two horses she loved. Jessie guided them carefully with the four leather reins between his fingers on both hands, so as not to weed out any of the now unexpectedly valuable corn. He shifted his weight a little in the hard steel seat. The sun was high in the sky.

An approaching hum developed behind them, reaching a deafening crescendo overhead, making Jack jump a little to the left, pulling Jim over some too.

"Whoa Jim! Haw Jack! We're knocking corn down!" Gracie looked up and saw the two double winged planes roar by not far above. They were a matched set of Belgians, colored a dappled gray with white streaks on their tails and a white blaze on their faces. The planes were so close she could see the scarves wrapped around the pilots' necks blowing fiercely in the wind as the men sat in their open cockpits. The planes climbed in sharp arcs away from each other. At the top of their circles they dove and swooped down, barely missing each other as they crossed paths. Jessie blocked the sun with his hand so he could watch the show.

The horses stopped in their tracks, not being able to see

much due to their blinders and knowing they couldn't run off with their master.

"Dang it, can't they practice their acrobatic skills someplace else," Jessie lamented. *Though I guess maybe they'll protect my son from harm, wherever he's stationed in Europe,* he thought.

It had been a few months since he last received a letter from Floyd. Creased and smudged, the envelope that contained it was adorned with multiple postmarks and unusual stamps.
"I don't have much time to write, Dad and Mom, but I miss you and the farm so terribly. Much more terrible it is here, and that is all I will say other than I am still okay." He concluded, "Love Floyd."

"Gracie, we've just got to raise all we can this year. The world seems to need it bad. There's just not enough food right now. This war is so damn frustrating and sad." Gracie raised her eyebrows as she heard that word he'd never uttered in her presence before.

It's so absurd that we are going to make money on this suddenly high priced corn, due to the death and destruction from a war in Europe, he thought, as he paused and looked down between the reins at the ground behind Jack's huge feet. Jim's tail swished away a fly buzzing above his strong back and it fell to the ground in front of Jessie's eyes.

"Gracie, they call those pilots 'Flying Aces' given their daring and dangerous, bold efforts." She didn't say anything, but gazed motionless towards the horizon as the planes flew to the east out of sight. The dissonance of the engines faded away, and the solitude of the farmland returned.

"One day he'll come home, Gracie."

She walked back down the row a bit and tried to stand the few bent-over plants back up, pushing some dirt around them with her feet. *Maybe it will rain tonight and they'll be okay,* she thought.

Jessie and the Construction

Jessie was born in Ohio, before the turn of the century. It seems a long time ago to me, and far away. He was the son of a sharecropper farmer there in the river valley, which was a good place to farm. But land became scarce, and Jessie's father had several sons. At a young age, Jessie's father decided to strike out for a place they could own themselves. His father heard that farmland was cheap in Nebraska, so he loaded up their belongings and headed there. Jessie got the chance to buy the farm just south and a little east of town a few miles from the Elkhorn River, in Madison County.

He had little money but a business mind, so he borrowed funds from the local bank to get started. It wasn't after too many years of farming that Jessie was raising lots of things. He grew corn, oats, and alfalfa, which he rotated on the fields to keep them healthy and productive. He raised Angus cattle, Percheron horses, Duroc hogs, Shropshire sheep, and Rhode Island Red chickens. (I wish Evan would have raised chickens, since they would have been great fun to chase around!) This all took a lot of effort, and it was known that Jessie was a really hard worker.

Farming and raising livestock started getting really profitable. Jessie bought more land in the same home section he lived on. Corn and cattle prices were so good, he could he could pay for a farm in only a few years. So he borrowed some money and bought another piece of land. Part of this was due to a huge world war that caused a great need for food. Farmers in the United States were asked to grow more, to make up for European farmers who couldn't produce enough because the war was fought on their soil.

At the time, Jessie had one daughter named Gracie. She loved horses and was always in the pen where the draft horses stayed. She had befriended them and fed them oats out of her hand. Jim and Jack were their names, and her father had raised them. Her love for horses took on a tragic ending, though.

One afternoon, coming from town with the wagon and team, Jessie and his daughter turned in to the driveway of the farm. It was bumpy, and the team was excited to get back to the barn. They took off at a trot.

"Watch out, Gracie! Don't lean over the side!"

"Yes, sir,"

About that time, the wagon lurched, with the big wheel dropping into a rut on Gracie's side.

The spring seat launched her off, sending her headfirst ahead of the front wooden wheel.

"Gracie!" he yelled, as he reached out but unable to grab her.

"Papa", she screamed but only for a moment. The heavy wagon, loaded with supplies from town, rolled over her chest with the front wheel before Jessie could get the team to stop. She died right there, on the road, in her father's arms, as her mother ran out of the house to see what the commotion was about.

"My dear Gracie," she cried. "I can't live without you. You will always be my only daughter, and I will love you forever."

They buried her in the cemetery on the south edge of town.

Margaret soon fell into a deep depression. For days at a time, she would stay in bed. Jessie had to make his own food and serve her some to sustain his dear wife with her broken heart. Things had been going so well. They had everything they needed, yet they had lost their only daughter. At least they still had a son.

The old house Margaret lay in was not built very well, and was falling into disrepair. Jessie decided that building a new house for her might help bring her out of her sadness. Financially, he felt that things were going well enough that they could afford it. So Jessie hired a person to construct a grand home from a picture and plan he had seen in a book he'd bought in Northfork, some miles down the river valley. He had to borrow some of the money to pay for this home but foresaw no problem repaying it. Crops prices had been good and he even had some money for a down payment. It took two years before it was finished.

One morning, when the carpenters arrived to finish siding the house, they noticed some writing on the red tarpaper they had covered the sides with. There, on the north side, was the name *Gracie*, along with the date, scrolled in pretty handwriting.

The men found Jessie and showed it to him.

"Margaret must have gotten out of bed and wrote it!" he exclaimed, then stood back, looking at it mesmerized. Later when asked, she denied ever writing it.

So who did? He wondered.

Little did he know that, years later, in a remodel project by my master, it would be found again, like a time capsule of history and love, written in one word.

Time rolled on, and Jessie and Margaret moved into their handsome new home. Her depression had lifted after she saw the writing. She felt like a part of her little girl was still there, living with her in the new house.

The war was over, and Jessie's son Floyd, who had been a soldier in it, finally came home. He arrived from the west road, and when coming over the last hill, he saw the new house.

He asked the driver to stop the car on the road, took a pause, and then said softly, "Look what my father has built. There is not another around like it."

Once, when I was in the basement of the house, and I noticed shelving made from Floyd's crate that had carried his belongings back from far overseas. The wood still smelled musty, with the scent of the ocean, and of different lands. Floyd didn't talk much about the war, except to tell his Pa that "Compared to what I've seen, this is heaven here. No man should let war begin. Blessed and great are the peacemakers."

The next few crop seasons, things changed some on the farm. Crop and livestock prices were not as good as they had been. The weather was worse, too. Not enough rain, and hot summers, started getting more typical, so yields of corn and oats were less. Jessie had enough to feed his livestock, but not as much to sell. His bank account started going dry along with the weather.

Evergreen Stock Farm

Looking outwards one day, to the green fields of corn, oats and alfalfa, Jessie told Margaret, at his side on the front porch, "Let's name our place after the color I see today, and pray it will forever adorn our farm. I propose we call it Evergreen Stock Farm."

"You have a vision with a name now."

Well, I'm not sure about the "ever" part, and squirm a little as I think about them then, with all the hopes and dreams they had for the farm. But I do know the feeling, like the day the little girl Clara and I met.

"We'll grow plenty of livestock and I know it will be a happy place with green pastures for all who live here, Margaret."

The loamy dirt was black and deep, and the gently rolling hills provided for good drainage. All he needed to do was pay for it. There were endless things to do, though, such as building fences to keep cows and pigs from getting loose, along with caring for crops and doing chores.

But the good times began to wane, and troubles were mounting in the '20s. By 1923, Jessie wasn't able to pay the taxes on the farm. The next year, he couldn't either. Though he was sometimes still raising decent crops, the prices received for them couldn't pay all the bills. Decisions had to be made about who was going to get paid and who was not. Jessie took out another loan. And then another.

By the mid to late '20s, rainfall was less and crop yields got worse. Jessie had stopped sleeping well at night. He lay awake thinking of ways he could make the payments and pay the taxes. He wanted to provide well for his family but it just wasn't working out.

"Jessie, I don't think you better buy anything but your basic needs for the farm and family. You've got to start repaying some of this debt."

"Yes, sir, I understand, and have already cut things to the bone." Jessie replied.

"I've got a bank to run here, and I'm sorry it's this way," the banker replied, looking out the window to Main Street, then straight at Jessie.

The meeting ended with Jessie writing a small repayment check to the bank, not nearly paying off the loans.

Jessie was picking corn west of the house that day. He had begun harvest earlier in the month and was getting close to done. He wanted to make sure he got it put away before anything happened to it, and the weather was turning cold. He desperately needed all the money he could get for the excess, beyond what he needed to save to feed his hogs, cattle, sheep, and chickens. When he retired to the house that evening, after doing all the chores and milking the single milk cow they had to provide for them, he sat down to supper.

Margaret told him that a neighbor had stopped by after returning from town for supplies. The neighbor said news on the street was that the stock market had crashed in New York. Jessie didn't have any stocks but he knew this wasn't good for the country. He felt sorry for those that had lost money and were worried for the companies they owned or had an interest in by owning a share of their stock. He was becoming used to dealing with financial stress and having to explain to creditors that he was going to be late on payments.

They called it Black Friday. I don't know much about it but I know the stock market fell a whole lot. Where it fell from, I'm not sure, but I do know it got hurt. Things seemed to get broken, and then I heard people started going broke. Jessie was already having more trouble finding the money every six months to pay the loan on the house back to the bank.

"What's this all mean to us, Jessie?" Margaret asked him one night, while serving him some boiled potatoes and scrambled eggs, a typical home grown meal for them.

"I'm not sure but I will talk to our banker in Tilden in the morning," as he thought to himself, *Maybe we shouldn't have built this house,* gazing up at the beautiful oak woodwork in the living room. Jessie went down into the basement that night and turned off the power plant that provided lights for the home. This was an unusual thing to have in a farmhouse. Electricity had not come to rural areas yet so many people still had nothing but kerosene lamps. Jessie was progressive and had wired his new home for electricity when he built it, then installed the gas-powered generator to please Margaret. She had worked very hard all her life. The electricity was a significant pleasure, and the glow of the lamps in the house on the golden oak floors provided an ambiance that was calming each evening, athough now they ran them sparingly.

Lying in bed that night, Jessie thought of what might become of his blessed farm he had worked so hard on. *How upset will my banker be tomorrow? I hate these difficult situations. It was me that signed the loan, and I must follow through. I would expect no less.* Things were not good in the banking world as ripples spread from the fall of the stock market. I wonder how something crashing so far away could be felt here in Nebraska but I guess it was so. I'm aware of reverberations happening all the time.

Jessie thought, *I must make the best of this and tell my banker I will do everything I can to make the payments on the farm. He shouldn't worry, that is for me to do. Please don't let him sell me out.* So Jessie did his job and lay there all night, worrying. His mind raced with the possibilities of a farm sale, of having to leave the place, not knowing where to go or what to do. He thought of Margaret beside him, resting better since he hadn't told her all he knew about the financial situation yet. He thought of Floyd, his son the war veteran, who had hopes of taking over the farm when it was time for him to quit. He thought of his little girl Gracie riding the little pony they got for her in the farmyard the week before she died. How would he handle yet another personal loss?

Just before sun up, he slept for a little bit.

The Dirty Thirties

Jessie got through the meeting with the banker that next day. He wore his best suit. Before going in, he straightened his tie, and picked up his shoulders. The banker told him things were getting serious, and the bank was having problems with liquidity. I think of liquid as water but maybe it was about things flowing well with money. It seemed like both kinds were in short supply these days. Jessie went back to the farm and continued his work, caring for the livestock that fall and winter the best he could with what supplies he had.

I wish my cows would have wintered better. They sure look thin. Maybe the grass will grow quick.

The new decade arrived and the spring of 1930 had come, only this time sooner than what Jessie was used to. It was dry in the fields, so he planted the oats in early March and the corn in early May. The oats came up after a late-month snow had melted, providing some moisture to the dusty soil. By the time Jessie plowed and tilled the field, that moisture was gone. He decided to plant the corn in the dry dirt anyway and wait for a rain to moisten the seeds, allowing them to sprout. So he did and then waited. He waited out the month of May that was usually the best time to start a corn crop. It was nearly the first of June before the rain came and settled the dust that had been blowing for some days now.

"Honey, it's raining! It's coming down hard! We haven't had one like this since last year."

"Do we need to go downstairs, away from the lightning?" she murmured.

"I'll take my chances. I want to just lie here and listen to it rain with you."

Jessie sank into the feather bed that night as the thunderstorm rolled over the house. He saw the lightning strikes flash through the windows, and the following low boom of thunder rattling the windowpanes a bit. The smell of the rain coming through the open window was fresh, moist, cool, and simply heaven to a crop farmer like him.

In less than a week the corn sprouted yellow shoots and then emerged through the brown crust of soil. Leaves unfurled from the bright green tips a few days after that. Catching the warm sun they began the process of replication.

It's going to be a good stand, Jessie thought as he walked across the field west of the place two weeks later. *Miracles do happen.*

By late June, the plants were six inches tall. It had not rained any more than a sprinkle since early that month. The sun was beginning to bake the bare soil, and temperatures were rising quickly. Jessie was just finishing stacking his first cutting of hay from the alfalfa field. The sweat had run down his face as he worked his team of horses with a hay sweep attachment in front of them. He took another drink of water from his jug, looking up into the hot sun, wondering what the year was to bring for him.

The corn came up good, but will there be enough rain to raise a crop?

He needed a good harvest to make the payments and keep his lenders at bay. *Sad that raising a crop and livestock had to be about money. Shouldn't it be good enough to just raise grain and provide food for our country?* But he knew the reality was that it had to be about money, if he was going to feed his family and repeat the process next year.

Jessie's face was already weathered and creased. His hard hands were cracked, yet thick with muscle. They rested in a curled position, as if ready to grab and squeeze the next wrench or pitchfork. He came in that evening at sunset, which was nearly 10 P.M. that time of year.

"I got most of it done today, dear, but it was a lot to stack by myself." Bent over some from the day of pitching hay around to build the stack, he went to the kitchen sink to wash the dirt from his face. *I've got to keep going, keep trying. She needs this home, and I need hold this farm together,* he thought, as he splashed water on his face, and blindly reached for a towel hanging close by. The dream he had been chasing for so many years, was now under severe threat, given the Depression that had hit the nation.

That summer turned out to be pretty fair. The crop came in a bit smaller than the year before, but the price had dropped twenty-five percent. It was also less than half the nearly two dollars per bushel he had received fifteen years earlier when his house had been completed. But the next year things fell apart.

The spring of 1931 was dryer than the last. Jessie planted his crops again, but they suffered right from the onset. Soil moisture levels were depleted from the past years' crop sucking up every drop stored in the heavy clay earth. I've dug a badger out deeper than three feet in a corn field and still tore up wet dirt and roots. That's a lot of digging though, even in soft dirt. That year it would be up to whatever rain came to nourish the crops.

By June, things were serious. It only took Jessie a day to put up the hay crop since it hadn't grown much above his ankles. The good news was that it dried quickly in the hot sun, so it would store well in the barn after he pitched it off the hayracks to the grapple that hung over the pointed roof. Through a cable system hitched to horses, he could lift it to the haymow and drop it in the center of the second level. There it would be ready to feed the livestock in the winter by forking it down to the lower level. *I'll never get this full at this rate. What are my cows and horses going to eat this winter? Pray for rain every night, I guess.*

July was disastrous. Jessie's pasture dried up, so the cattle grazed with noses close to the   ground, moving forward all the time. He turned the cows out in the road ditches to eat any available forage there. The hogs suffered from the heat, so he pumped water into their yard to make mud holes for them to lie in. *I hope nothing goes wrong with the well in this weather.* Jessie used the jack handle to pump water for the livestock on the few days that the wind didn't blow dry and hot from the south, and his wooden storage tank went empty.

In early August, a cloudbank developed late one evening to the west. Soon lighting flashed overhead but only a few teasing sprinkles hit the ground.

By September, the crop was turning brown.

In early October, he harvested what little corn there was. The ears had shriveled to less than half their normal size and many plants were barren. *Damn, I threw that one clear over the wagon again. Nothing works the same this year; nothing goes right. I'm a failure.* Even when the ears hit the target, they didn't make the typical thud against the bang board of the wooden wagon.   Instead, the fluff of the loose shucks allowed a small whoosh to be heard as they hit and slid to the pile inside.   It took less time to harvest all the corn that year, only for having to empty fewer wagons, though he walked the same many miles to get it done. The corn crib on the farm ended up less than half full that year.

Next spring, the neighbors came over as customary to help him shell out the little remaining corn which hadn't already been fed over the winter to the hogs and steers in the pens.

"Boy, Jessie, this isn't going to take long," as his neighbor with a grim face looked at the dwindling crib of corn.

Jessie stood mute. *You don't have to tell me that.*

He took the few wagonloads to the grain company in town four miles away. The price paid for each bushel was also half of what it was the year before.

* * * * *

The next couple of seasons, things went from bad to terrible. Crops and prices both were lower than low. Jessie kept working and trying and hoping. He shipped some sheep he had raised to market at the Omaha Stockyards. The sheep were loaded on a railcar in Tilden where there was a place to board them, and a loading chute that allowed them to walk up a ramp into the car when it showed up. He hoped that they would bring more in Omaha and earn him some money to pay the overdue bills. He had done his best to grow the lambs up but, with limited grass and short crops, the sheep weren't as fat as they should have been.

He waited for the check to come in the mail from the Stockyards. An envelope finally came a few weeks later. There was no check. Instead, a note and invoice explained that the sheep had brought so little that they had not fully paid the shipping, feed bill, and sales commission. So they kindly asked Jessie to send them money for what was still owed. Jessie fell back into his chair, thinking, *Oh my God, how much worse can it get?*

I'll fix 'em, and penned a letter back to the stockyard company. In it he stated that he had no money to pay them. But he had a few more sheep he could ship! He chuckled to himself with this thought, a sarcastic joke that gave him a bit of reprieve from the threat to his farm that so often overcame him.

Jessie walked down the driveway with his now thirty-year-old son, back from months away at a job on a farm in Missouri where it rained more. They talked about the situation of the farm and finances.

"I don't know what more I can do, Pa,"

"There is little you can do. Just keep bringing back some grocery money when you can."

"Pa, I wish I had enough money to bail you out from this darn debt on the farm,"

"But, Floyd, it's not your problem, it's mine. I made the situation. I should have never built that house and indebted the farm so much. Things looked so bright then, and your mother deserved something special. There are nice homes in the city, why can't we have one right here? I sure work hard enough."

"There was a man down in Missouri, who, while leaning on a shovel, told me that if hard work made one rich, then he had a mule that was a millionaire."

"I know, Floyd. It's not all about hard work. I've tried to play my business cards right but the deck looks stacked against me. I've never told you this before, son, but the reason my father and I came to Nebraska is because he lost his farm in Virginia. It was tough going there; poor soil and low crop prices. All he would say to me about it was to never borrow too much money. When's this cycle ever going to end?"

Jessie thought of his little girl that Margaret had borne and then lost so soon. She had lived with that brokenness all these years. *She keeps standing by my side. I can't believe how she does all her work, cares for me, and smiles some when the sunset is turning hues of pink, or when she looks up at the stars on a summer night.*

It seemed memories of the curly-locked girl, skipping down the same driveway on the farm, lifted her even during these days of drought and despair.

"Do you remember when I let her jump in the horse tank that hot summer day?" she asked.

"I do. Then I remember her swinging on the rope swing by the house, to dry off in the warm breeze."

At least the woman I love has a fine home to live in and enjoy. But now, some days, the blowing dust sifted through the windows and doors, leaving a layer on the smooth wood floors. She endlessly cleaned, ensuring that her husband would have a place to come home to that was kept and ready for him to retire in each evening. As the wind storms from the south got worse, the dust problem did so as well. Jessie and Margaret were both developing a chronic cough.

Setting Suns on One Farm

Sunsets on Evergreen Stock Farm were special. To the west of the farm, there was a splendid horizon of rolling, hilly fields. To the far north, there was the Elkhorn River Valley with its towering cottonwood trees, then a vast panoramic boundary between land and sky. On the horizon there was a large cut made between two hills where massive herds of buffalo used to come to the river for water. To the west, when the sun dropped low, the blue changed to hues of pinks, oranges, and reds, in sweeping horizontal lines, all blended in. On clear days, some of them had to be God's art pieces. Sometimes to the east, he would watch a thunderstorm cloudbank, with high billowing clouds, move away after drenching his farm. Then, rarely, a full rainbow would form.

Jessie always tried to stop work and look at sunsets for a moment. *My gift from my Creator for a hard day's work maybe.* On Sundays, when he tried not to work and just did the necessary chores, he would sit on the west porch of the house with Margaret and ponder, while enjoying another setting take place. Only once the sun was fully down would he rise and go in the house. The evenings were quiet there, with only the lowing of cows heard by his family, or a few coyotes in the distance howling and barking as they readied for the nighttime activities of a more nocturnal species.

"These are the good moments, aren't they, Margaret?" Jessie would say. She would just look over at him and smile.

In the back of his mind, though, was always the haunting pressure of the failing finances of their beloved farm. Things had got so serious; his banker had asked him to sell the farm to pay the loan off. The bank was worried about a thing called solvency. I think that was related to liquidity thing. It seems to me the bank was worried for its survival as well. So it had to put pressure on farmers like Jessie to find a way to make good on their loans.

Jessie spoke to Margaret one evening, while on the porch.

"We can't just give in to the bank's wishes, Margaret. I'm not a quitter."

"Jessie, you have given your life for this place and built such a farm. I'm with you through this fight with not only nature and drought, but with the forces that might make us lose this farm."

The next day, Jessie went into town and told the banker he wouldn't sell, that the next year had to be better, and he should hang on with hope, just as Jessie was. The banker was not pleased.

By 1936, Jessie had already been served a notice by the county sheriff that his farm was in legal foreclosure, and it was to be sold at auction at the courthouse. This took time to go through all the legal channels. Jessie had hired an attorney to represent him and Margaret in the court action. Like wrangling with a young horse that needed to be broken, Jessie was now wrapped up in a court fight to save his farm somehow. The debt was large, and the law strong. Jessie and Margaret had signed the papers for the original loan and were obligated.

"I just need more time, your honor. Things have been really tough, you know."

The judge paused then lifted his head up slowly.

"I understand but there's nothing in these loan documents that take that into consideration, Mr. Jessie."

The court quickly ruled in favor of the bank. There were more farmers waiting in the hall, with the same problems.

I know well the level of despair that rose up in Jessie and Margaret. The winter was going to be cold, and made colder by the fact that the farm might be sold by then. Options had run out for them legally.

There's one more chance, if we can use the newly passed law. Jessie paced the house floors that night, hoping it would work, or they would have to move.

In September, the farm was sold at auction to the highest bidder on the Madison County Courthouse steps. The Fremont Joint Stock Land Company bought the farm. Jessie and Margaret did not go to the auction. Their attorney did, though. After the sale, he filed a motion to nullify the sale because of a congressional action that had taken place in 1934, postponing the sale of a farm under foreclosure for five years. Jessie's attorney, filed for such protection, and the farm sale was stopped. For the moment, Jessie and Margaret still owned their farm.

* * * * *

The winter of 1936-1937 was a long one. The corn crop that fall was another disaster. All that was harvested were a few ears from the low areas that had a little more moisture in the soil. They preserved this tiny little bit in jars as table corn to eat. It seemed, during these dry years, the winters were more severe than normal. Given the worries on the farm of shortages of feed for livestock, along with worries of properly feeding themselves, it made the winter even longer.

When spring came, Jessie still was hopeful for hope was all he had. He had decided to finish an old project, building a yard fence around the house, which involved forming and pouring concrete for nicely designed corner posts. *I've got all the materials I bought years ago so I might as well get it done. Margaret will be glad when I do.* He dug deep holes for the posts to fill with cement and gravel. He built the forms on the ground, then placed scrap iron rods and shafts upright to strengthen the structure. The posts would rise about four feet tall. A mechanical mixer, driven by a tractor, was used to mix the cement, gravel, and water mixture. There was a turning power takeoff shaft hooked in between the units. It still was a lot of work.

Jessie was working alone that day. It was a Saturday, and the week had been long. He poured the last post on the south side of the house. In a hurry, he stepped over the driveshaft to save a little time. It was unguarded; just a fast spinning piece of steel. The overalls he wore touched the shaft when he stumbled. Like lightning, he was grabbed and thrown to the ground. The tough material wound up on the shaft quickly and tore some of it from him. His leg was pulled in, and the steel dug into his thigh. Jessie grabbed for the tractor seat above to pull himself from the danger, but not soon enough to protect him from an injured, bleeding leg. Screaming, "Margaret, help!", he dragged himself to near the back porch and collapsed.

"Oh, my Lord!" she cried while latching on to her husband and helping him into the house, quickly grabbing some kitchen towels to wrap around the gaping wound in his thigh.

"I'm sorry, Margaret, it just happened so fast," lamented Jessie. He gritted his teeth and grabbed the armrest of the chair as she pressed hard on the wound to stop the bleeding.

"Hold it right there, Jessie, while I go for help." Margaret started the truck and headed for the neighbors just down the road.

"Jessie has been hurt badly! Please go to town and get the doctor so I can get back to help him!" she cried.

While she was gone, Jessie held on to his leg and the wrap, as blood still dripped to the floor. More tightly, he held on to the hope that this bad turn of events did not further risk his farm. *Who would care for the livestock, and how would he get the crops planted? How could this happen, after all Margaret and I have gone through on the farm?*

He hung on.

I'm sure his dog must have been pacing outside the door, fretting on his boss. In an hour or so, the doctor came. He cleaned and dressed the wound after working to no avail to close it. There was just too much flesh gone. He worried about the risk of infection since it had happened outside, with livestock and dirt all around. He could only hope and offer sulfa medication to ward it off, as penicillin was not available yet.

"This is a serious wound, Margaret," the doctor said. "We must tend to it daily for a long time, and keep Jessie in bed. Hopefully, it will get better."

Jessie was prayerful with those words, as he lay there that night with Margaret at his side. She had set up a bed in the front parlor, since he wasn't able to climb the stairs to reach the bedroom.

Outside, the wind blew, rattling the windows, only adding to the unsettled feeling inside. Otherwise, it was quiet as

Margaret sat in the chair beside her husband. There, she had a porcelain bowl with some water so she could dab his forehead as Jessie lay in a sweat. He dozed off in exhaustion though pain soon woke him.

"I love you, Margaret. Are we nearing the end?"

"I love you too, Jessie."

The morning came, and then another, and another. By then the sweats were bad, as fever set in. The doctor had come every day but this day Jessie seemed worse. His leg had turned a different color from the wound on down, a dark red, which the doctor told Margaret was a severe infection of the limb. He knew this risked the man's life and he might have to take drastic action the next day.

Jessie and Margaret had hoped that he could get better at home, thus avoiding a hospital stay, since they didn't have the funds to pay for it. Their resources had been wiped out by the Depression, drought, and nearly no income from crops or livestock. They did not want to incur any more debt that they might not be able to pay. So they hoped.

The next morning the doctor came and could see that Jessie's condition had gone from bad to worse. He had come prepared with a bag of tools for the ugly task at hand.

"Is the corn crop harvested? I've got to get up and go now, Doctor", he said, as Margaret wiped the sweat from his face.

"It's barely spring, Jessie, and you don't even have a crop planted."

The small town doctor had learned to deal with whatever situation arose. Today, he must take Jessie's leg off, in the hope of saving the man. Jessie was moved into the kitchen and placed on the cleaned table covered with a white bed sheet. Then he was put to sleep with some ether the doctor placed on a cloth and covered his nose and mouth with. A neighbor, who happened to be a midwife, assisted the doctor with the procedure.

In the front room outside the parlor, Jessie's son held his mother's hand while they waited. It was a cloudy, drizzly day near the end of March. No leaves had come out, and only a few sprigs of green grass were apparent in the house yard. The cement mixer sat quiet by the last post.

They moved Jessie back to the bed in the parlor after the surgery. He lay there for the next week, working hard to recover. In a delirium some of the time, he tried to process what was unfolding. *I've lost my leg but I must get well so I don't lose the farm too,* as his mind cleared a little.

Margaret stayed at his side every moment she could, while Floyd took care of the livestock chores outside. Jessie didn't get any better that week.

Three weeks to the day of the amputation, Jessie's wife, son, and the doctor were at his side. Two neighbor ladies were in the kitchen preparing food in hopes of somehow easing the pain that the family was going through. That late day in April was more sunny and warm.

Jessie succumbed to his injuries that afternoon.

His era had ended. The farm's challenges were over, at least for him. No more would he see the sun rise warm over his farm as he did the morning chores, or watch it set as he came in from the fields to an awaiting wife with a good supper on the table. He had left his beloved farm.

The only solace for Jessie was that it was still there.

Jessie was buried only a few miles to the northwest near town, overlooking his farm fields to the south. I've seen his headstone on one of my ventures about, and paused there a bit. A sense of the farm seems to linger there yet.

In August of 1937, his son Floyd wasn't able to hold off the sale of the farm anymore. He allowed the bank to move forward with foreclosure proceedings. The farm was sold on the Madison County Courthouse steps that September. The Fremont Joint Stock and Trust became the new owners of the farm, being its creditors. The farm, so beloved and cared for by Jessie, was now gone from his family.

A bank would own the farm now; every fence, board, and building, including the house. The livestock and machinery would be sold at auction. Margaret would have to move their possessions from her beloved home, and find a place to live in town.

New Owners, New Times

Some more years passed. The dust settled on the times, and on Jessie's grave. Then frequent rain finally washed it away, turning it back into productive soil. New life began springing up, including a new life for those living in agriculture. The house that had sat empty, found new occupants.

Homer and Nancy first rented the farm from the bank, not being able to afford to purchase it from the trust company. Soon, though, prices for corn, cattle, and hogs had risen to profitable levels. There had risen a new demand for food, out of a terrible situation; another World War they called Two. After what Floyd had told about One, I hate to think about it.

"Let's buy it, Nancy. The bank has offered us good terms, and I think we can pay it off in a few years," Homer said one night over the supper table.

"Let's do it!" she replied. "I love this home, and want to live here all my years with you." The deal was made, the papers signed in a few weeks. The crops grew well that year, while prices advanced even more. A first payment on the farm was made easily the next year.

Homer was a good manager. This was made easier by profit, and thus the ability to invest in better machinery, quality livestock, and quality seed. His farm produced in abundance - lots of fat cattle, big hogs, corn, oats, and alfalfa hay. There was plenty of food for the family; milk, chickens, and eggs, along with garden produce that was canned in the summer for the long winter months.

"The corn yields are great this fall, son! That new variety of seed corn sure is good!" Homer exclaimed.

"And the price posted at the elevator is good too, Daddy."

Government farm programs that helped farmers manage production as a whole, and stabilize prices to fair levels, seemed to be working. It was called the Agricultural Stabilization and Conservation Service of the United States Department of Agriculture.

"I guess after what happened in the Dirty Thirties, and now with a war going on, our country decided that it was in the best interests of our citizens to make sure we had a strong and productive system of agriculture, since no one wanted to go back to food shortfalls and Depression economics," Homer told Nancy one day, after visiting the local ASCS office. "They've increased support prices for corn and oats to better levels!" Homer did not go off to war, like many of the men his age. He was needed to grow food for the masses of people who did not have the ability to do so themselves, so he was given a deferment. I don't know his dog's name but I bet he was happy!

Instead, Homer bought a new mechanical corn picker. Before, it had been harvested by hand. Each ear had to be stripped from the stalk and thrown into a wagon alongside the row. A team of horses, which responded to voice commands, walked alongside, pulling the wagon.

"Gee!" he would holler to his horses to move left.

"Haw!" he would call to ask them to turn right.

The process took months then, since there were up to fifteen thousand ears to be harvested on each acre. *I can harvest it all in a few weeks now, and all I have to do is push the clutch in and turn the steering wheel. Pay for it, though.* Homer thought. The mechanized corn picker was pulled by a John Deere tractor. It had a two-cylinder engine, so it had a slow turning, popping sound coming from the exhaust. Thus, it got the nickname "Johnny Popper".

We dogs sure enjoyed being out in those fields with the horses for months at a time. We could still follow the tractors but this was more dangerous and noisy. Many a dog lost their tails in power takeoffs or even their lives by being run over by a big wheel! I sure stay away from farm equipment these days!

They raised so much corn and oats that he needed a better place to store it. So Homer built the modern granary that held two thousand four hundred bushels of grain overhead, and four thousand bushels of ear corn in cribs below. That way he didn't have to haul the bushels to the local grain company in town, in the midst of the busy harvest time.

Homer loved raising cattle. He especially liked to feed calves to full growth, and ready them to be sold at auction somewhere for beef. He used the corn and alfalfa he grew to accomplish this. Dogs like to eat a little shelled corn once in a while, especially if they're really hungry, but we never eat alfalfa! That's left for cows, sheep and horses.

Homer's son was named Donald. He grew up on the farm, like many farm boys, at his father's side. He learned how to drive the John Deere tractors at an early age. His "daddy", as Donald always called his father, would have him plow the fields with another Johnny Popper they owned. Donald could be seen on that seat, in spring, whistling to the dog trotting along, and singing a song. Soon the fields would be ready to plant the spring crops in, after a few more passes with a disk and harrow. That's how they did it in those days.

Donald grew up, got married, and lived on a farmhouse to the east of the big house Jessie had built. He worked on the farm and held a job in town during those years. Crop prices had soured, and farm programs were being pressured to reduce the price supports. The farm was now not large enough to support both families, so Donald supplemented his income from work at the local car garage in town. He raised one son with his wife, Harriet.

"Did you see the price of the four cylinder John Deere tractor, Daddy? It's more than we get for a crop of corn!"

They drove on through the implement dealer's lot in town. Homer always had a pen of cattle he was fattening for market. He would smile to see them, just south of the barn, in their pen near the concrete silo that had been built long ago by Jessie. The structure held fodder for livestock during the winter as well. It was placed in there to ferment so as not to spoil, and turn even tastier for the bovines that ate it. When hauled out in a wagon to the feed bunks, it would steam on a cold winter morning, mixing with the foggy breath of the animals hovering over it.

On hot summer days, though, Donald could be found mowing the hay down and allowing it to dry for some time before it was raked into windrows to be baled. He helped with all the field work. When it came time to bale the dried and ready-to-store alfalfa, it took two men - one driving the tractor and baler, and the other stacking the bales on the hayrack pulled in tow behind the machines. It was a demanding job, keeping up with the green, wire-tied bales being expelled up a short chute to the front of the hayrack. Then they were carried back and stacked in tiered fashion, sometimes above a man's head high. One hundred and fifty bales could reasonably be stacked on a typical wagon.

On the east side of the steer yard was a feed rack made of wooden planks that allowed cattle to reach through and eat hay that was thrown to them twice a day. This is where the alfalfa bales were stacked in the summer, in preparation for a pen of cattle to consume them in early fall. Homer enjoyed haying the cattle each morning and evening. Nancy could even observe him through the glass in the kitchen door to the west. The cattle would see him on the pile of neatly stacked bales and line up against the feed rack with their heads through to get the first bites of hay thrown to them.

"Watch out, calves!" he would cry, as he rolled the sixty-pound bales down to them, each bouncing from tier to tier. He cut the wire that held them together after they arrived. *More fence repair supplies*, he thought, as he folded the wire tight. Then he spread them out so each animal could have his share. There was a pecking order, of course; with the most aggressive animal making sure it was in the right position to get all it could of the sweet-smelling, pungent, still-green hay.

I suppose there's a pecking order for farmers and farms too. I wonder how this place stacks up, Homer thought, as he saved the wire in a barrel by the barn.

* * * * *

It was the year 1961and John Kennedy was president. He was also dealing with something called "The Bay of Pigs" which was a pretty serious situation for humans and dogs alike. Life or death for humanity, I heard. This doesn't make much sense to me, since pigs are usually put in pens and not found in any bays. In any case, it seemed like life and death was at the helm on the farm then too.

That day, Homer was haying the steers that had recently been put in the yard adjoining the pile of hay bales. It had been a long hot summer, and he had not been feeling good. His energy had been lower than he was used to, and his breath shorter than he liked. That evening was sweltering, a latent summer evening even though the calendar had switched from August. *I sure am sweating a lot,* he thought. He was on his twelfth bale when it occurred. It struck him hard in the chest. He dropped the bale, and fell to his knees. Grabbing the place near the pocket that carried his tidy pen holder, he called out.

"Nancy, come help me! Donald, come quick!" he cried. *They can't hear me.*

He was low, on the other side of the still large hay pile. So there was no response. The pain was sharp, and his breath stopped. Falling facedown, he rolled towards the rack and landed on his back in the hay he just spread out for the cattle to consume.

Quiet now, Homer whispered, "Donald, please take care of the farm for me".

His animals backed away in surprise. Then slowly, curiously, the steers again breached the wide opening between the planks and peered at their unmoving owner. They pushed and shoved each other. As one moved back, another moved forward in a process that allowed many of them to smell of something wrong. It was quiet, other than their breath pulling in the scent and then exhaling for another. Their ears went back in concern each time they picked it up.

Soon, all who had desired a glimpse of the happening had their turn. Then, in an unusual fashion, the cattle moved to the edges of the rack, instead of the normal middle, and resumed feeding. Homer lay alone now, his head and body resting on a bed of soft hay, with the smell of summer drifting up perfuming his still body and maybe even carrying his soul upward to his maker. The few steers at the back of the pen, who had no room at the bunk bawled mournfully.

* * * * *

Donald knew his father would want him to try to carry on. He did the best he could to fulfill Homer's wishes though he never got to say goodbye to him or hear his last request. But he knew, maybe since it was just something that had to be done. He planted the crops and cared for the livestock that was left.

Donald's son, Jeb, was beginning to be good help. Jeb liked the farm, and stayed near it as much as he could.

"Jeb, the tractor engine is missing, and I need it to run to feed the cows with the wagon."

"Ok, Dad."

Then later, "It runs good now, Dad. The distributor needed adjusting."

"Could you feed the cows with it, Jeb? I've got to get to work in town."

"Sure, Dad."

When Donald asked something, Jeb would simply do it. He had a good heart and a mild manner. With rumpled hair, and a well-worn and overly dirty barn jacket, he typically reserved his words. Sedate, he seemed to know something unspoken about the farm and its history. There was a sort of melancholy in him. He was always doing something for someone else. Sometimes his good nature was taken advantage of. He didn't seem to mind. He just did as requested, and he didn't ask questions.

Donald's mother was now getting old and needed more care. So he moved Nancy to the farmhouse with Harriet. This left the place to the east for the now-grown young man Jeb to live in. It was a much lesser house, and stood quietly a half-mile east of the dwelling Jessie built. It was white too, and had a screened-in porch on the south side. A bit dilapidated, yet still quite functional, Jeb had hopes to fill it someday.

The Auctioneer's Cry

Twenty years had passed since Homer had died on the farm. Working the farm with the tools and equipment his father had left him, Donald, and now his son, had held it together to this point. Donald had kept his job, since it helped supplement their income through lean years. But this wasn't always good for the farm. Crops still were planted but later than they should have been, and the weeds sometimes got away and grew with them. Before, in the era of his father, the fields were kept clean with timely cultivation of the corn.

Now Donald called the shots, many times after work in town and when the light was getting low in the west. This just didn't leave enough time. Jeb would sometimes wait all day, wondering what was best to do first. By the time his orders were given, it was too late. Jeb was a good car mechanic. He loved cars and had a special one that he tinkered with all day, while he was waiting. Sometimes a neighbor would stop over and ask him to look at a problem with their car.

"Dad, I made twenty bucks today fixing a car. I think I'll go to town this Saturday night and see a movie."

"That's good, Jeb. Your mother and I are kind of short on grocery money this week. Do you suppose you could loan me that twenty?"

"Of course."

Jeb would have the cultivator on the tractor and ready to go, but Donald would step-in.

"We better hold off, Jeb. It's supposed to rain this week, and we wouldn't want the weeds to come back to life, by a saving rain. Why don't you give it a week."

"Alright, Dad."

But they'll be too big to kill by next week, he thought.

The following week he cultivated, and could hardly see the rows for the fast growing weeds covering the ground in between. *I'll do what I can, but this is miserable.*

The fields showed it, by fall, with the corn only shoulder high.

"The banker says we've got to raise more, Jeb."

"Maybe irrigating the crops would help. Everybody around is drilling wells, Dad; why not us?"

"I guess we should. It costs a bunch, though. I'll see what the banker says about a loan."

"Then we'll need more grain storage too," Jeb replied. "The granary isn't near enough anymore. I guess you should ask about a loan for some new steel bins too."

"Ok, I'll stop in before I go to work at the gas station tomorrow."

Wells offer a farm, and a dog, an abundance of cold, crystal clear water supplied by irrigation systems using pipes and sprinklers. The water tastes good, and whenever it runs freely on the ground in the summer, I take the chance to lie in it! (Then I can cool my furry belly while also lapping some of the cold pleasure up!) Donald installed irrigation systems to connect to the wells, which allowed the crops to be watered when rainfall did not come. How great this could have been fifty years earlier, when the dust clouded out the sun some days.

Donald had to borrow a sum of money to install the two wells and systems. His farm had gone up in value. Land prices had increased to historically high levels in the past few years. The cost of borrowing money was high at the time. But Donald knew it would make his farm more valuable and more productive. The papers were signed, the investment made, and the wells drilled deep, deep into the ground. And Donald went deep, deep into debt for the first time. Jessie's old farm, now owned by Donald's family, was mortgaged again. The lien was filed with the same courthouse that the farm had been sold at years ago.

The water flowed cold, clear, and abundant, as Donald and Jeb had envisioned. It was a pretty dry year, that year, so they were lucky they could irrigate the crops. But the weeds grew, too - especially a nasty one called cane, which was difficult to control, and grew from its roots time after time if you cut it off or tried to spray it with a weed killer.

The cane did well under irrigation, and then towered over the corn shading it out from the sun. Since corn needs lots of sunlight to grow, it suffered from this. Then the cane produced heads with lots of tall black seeds that hung heavy when maturing in the fall. When Donald and his son went to harvest the crops, the cane heads were shattered and fell to the ground, there in waiting for the next spring to grow and produce even more cane and less corn on the fields.

It didn't take many years of this for the bills started going unpaid—including the loan at the bank. This wouldn't have been so bad with poor crops and all, since Donald did raise some. But the price for corn was not good. There was an oversupply again in the country, and bins were full of this great resource. I don't see how too much food is bad, since I always want more. But I guess for a farmer who is supposed to live by the laws of supply and demand, too much isn't good. There seems there should be a better way .... I'm pretty sure this has all happened several times before in history. Not enough, then too much. Boom, then bust.

Donald liked to go to farm auctions and look at all the equipment. The ladies usually set up a food stand in a garage, or sometimes a food trailer was on hand. He liked to stop and get his cup of coffee, then go talk to fellow farmers.

"This is the third sale I've been to lately," he told the neighbor standing by him.

"I guess the bank is getting nervous, and selling a few guys out," the neighbor replied.

"I'm doing more with my banker, the one with more branches. They seem to be not as worried," he replied.

"I gotta tell you, that's the one selling out this farm," the neighbor said.

"Oh."

It wasn't long and the bank started becoming harsh with Donald, asking him to pay up. The loan originally had good collateral, given the high value of Donald's farm. But now things had changed, and the price of farm ground was going down. He was late on payments. Donald spoke to his son on that day: "They want us to pay it all back right now," he said.

"How are we going to do that?" Jeb replied.

"We could sell all the grain we have in the two new bins."

"But corn prices are cheap Dad, and it's got all that cane seed mixed in with it, so it will bring even less."

"We don't have any choice, so start hauling it to the grain company, and we'll see if it will be enough."

It wasn't near enough. The bins weren't full from last year's crop. Worse yet, it had spoiled some in storage, since they hadn't learned how to manage the aeration systems. So, there would be a discount taken for the damage to the kernels of grain.

The fall turned to winter, and the winter turned to spring. Donald tried to renew his loans and get operating money to pay for seed, fertilizer, and fuel to plant the next crop. But the bank kept delaying and asking for more paperwork, more security, and payment on the last year's loans.

"I'll be able to pay the operating loan back this fall, with all the crops I raise now that we have irrigation," he told the banker.

"But Donald, you had irrigation last year and the crops weren't any good."

"I know that. Darn shatter cane got ahead of us. This year will be different."

"Sure," the banker replied with a kind smile. "But, you've got loans, loans, and more loans."

It was planting season, as May rolled around; typically a bright time on the farm. The crops had to be planted that month for an optimum yield, since Nebraska has a short growing period, and there is just enough sunlight and heat to make a crop of corn. Donald had not raised the funds to either pay the loan or satisfy the bank, nor had he raised a loan to raise the crop.

"The loan is about through, so could you please get me the hundred bags of seed I ordered," Donald told the salesman over the telephone that morning.

"I've got to have a check before I can deliver the corn seed to you," the dealer stated.

"Alright."

Donald went to work in town that day, not knowing what to do. There he changed tires, and oil in a few cars, using the work to keep him from thinking of his situation.

Coming home that night he found his son, working on another car.

"Jeb, we can't continue. The bank is foreclosing on us, and if we don't sell now, no one will be able to get a crop planted on it in time."

"But Dad, all I want to do is farm all my life. How will I now, if we sell it?"

"I don't know."

* * * * *

By this time, Evan had a good farm operation developing. He was younger than even Jeb. He had first rented a piece of land from his father, and then found another on his own. He had a good lender who was helping him learn the business of finance. That winter he had the opportunity to rent a farm across the road from Donald's.

Evan was working across the road in a shed the day Jeb walked in. I wasn't even in the picture yet. It was a rainy day during planting season.

Jeb walked up to him. His head was down until he stopped a few steps away.

"It's not going good on the other side of the road," Jeb said. "The banker just told my dad he has to sell out."

"Oh no!" Evan said.

"We were hoping to plant just one more season but it seems that isn't going to happen. There's no seed to even plant."

"I hate it for you, Jeb."

My young Evan hated the notion of a farmer being sold out, and he knew the sadness of the situation. He knew farm prices were much too low for some farmers to make it, and it wasn't their fault. Instead, it was the fault of a system that was out of balance, that didn't work very well, and that wasn't ensuring a good price for valuable farm production. I wonder why it should be that way. Dogs love to be rewarded for what they do. I always like a pat when I do something right. And, when I catch something small to eat; well that rewards me too. It's a way dogs were made to survive. I guess all Jeb wanted to do was survive.

As tough as it was in farming, Evan still knew there were opportunities, if he was willing to take some risk. He knew he needed a home base that he owned if he was going to be successful at farming. He knew that there was nothing he could do about Donald and Jeb's situation, other than to console Jeb.

"I'm sorry, Jeb. We've been fighting the unfairness of this damn situation but we've lost so far."

Summer was just around the corner. As usual, the winter before had frozen things up. After the cold gray days of early spring, some things didn't come back alive. I don't know why Mother Nature would let that happen.

But she does.

Evan went to the realtor who was handling the sale of Donald's farm and considered the price being offered. It was terribly low, given what it had been worth just a few years before. *Will land values go even lower?* Evan wondered. *How would I get a loan to buy it? How would I find a way to pay for it, with prices being so low?* The questions went on. *Is it right for me to even buy the farm?* He put an offer in on the place just a little bit lower than the asking price. Later on same day Jeb had stopped by.

Who else is going to want to buy this farm? What's Jeb going to say to me tomorrow if we meet? He wondered, and didn't sleep much that night.

Within a few days, and after a plenty of negotiations, Donald accepted the final offer. It was just exactly enough to pay off his loans and free the farm from the bank's liens placed at the county courthouse. Within a few short weeks, and just in time to get it planted, that farm sale was closed with Evan. Donald, Harriet and Nancy were still living in the house. Evan and Jeb didn't talk much through that time. Lying in bed that night he wondered, *Did I really do the right thing? Can I ever even pay for it, if it is? If not, I'll be the third one to fail.*

Part of the terms of the sale was that Donald, Harriet, and Nancy could live on the farm for a time while they got things in order. Donald began the process of lining up an auction to sell the many, many pieces of farm machinery, tools, equipment, and even household items that he would no longer need. It was another year before the sale would be held.

The auction day was in March, not very sunny, but not too cold. The pickups lined the roadways coming to the farm, with over a hundred buyers coming to watch the auctioneer sell every piece, one by one. Much of it had been lined up in rows in the grassy area just east of the house. In the house yard, rows of furniture and wares were also lined up. A feed bunk held boxes of books and other unwanted goods, including some of Donald's parent's belongings.

The auctioneer worked off a pickup that drove along the items with farmers crowded around it. He sat in a big box with windows all around, and used a microphone and speaker system that blared out into the crowd.

"Boys, it's a big box on that wagon, and everything looks right. Before you know it you'll need one, and you'll wish you'd placed a bid! It doesn't look very used and look at those new tires! Why it's almost like new!"

Most of the farmers seemed unnerved by his banter.

"I'm bidding one hundred dollars, do I hear one-fifty, give me one-fifty, do I hear one seventy-five? Yeah! I do, give me two hundred now! Yup, yup, yup, give me two-fifty! Are you all done? One more time! Three hundred! Going, going gone! Sold for two seventy-five. Sir, you got a good deal, thank you everyone, it goes to bidder number twenty-five!"

The pickup moved forward to the next item, a wagon used to feed cow hay and silage next. "Boys, look at this good piece of machinery! Why, it looks almost new! Boys, don't wait long to bid, I've got lots to go! How about one thousand dollars, let's start there!" Some of the farmers were studying the rusty spot, missing paint and broken iron on the side of it.

"Do I hear fifteen hundred dollars? No? Well, how about twelve hundred? Yeah! I heard it, now thirteen hundred! Yeah! Thank you, sir! Yeah! I hear fourteen hundred! Young man, will you go one more time for fifteen hundred? Okay, yup, yup, yup, I got it! Going once, going twice—sold to the highest bidder! Thank you, son. You got a great deal. Bidder fifty-eight is the buyer."

Later, Evan, who was watching all this, asked the auctioneer how many were bidding on that wagon. He laughed and said, "Son, it was me and him all the way."

They were selling tools out of the old small wooden shop building when Evan walked up and stood by Donald. They had got along well through the past year. They spoke while they watched the items come out of the shed. Neighbors were helping set things onto the hayrack placed outside the door. The auctioneer stood on it and cried out his song above the crowd all around.

Suddenly, Donald broke down in tears. They flowed down his face and dripped on his pocketed shirt with pens and pencils in a protector stuffed inside. His brimmed ball cap was tipped up and to the side a little, as he always wore it. His eyes shone wet and glistening in the light that day. Soon, Donald came out of it and went back to hiding his emotions among the group all around. Evan slowly walked away as the speakers blasted out the sound of the auctioneer in a deafening, mesmerizing call to buy and bid just one more time. The auctioneer—and the forlorn cry of another farmer lost. *This seems so much more unfair than me having to leave my warm nest in Oklahoma. At least I was moving forward. Where are Donald, Harriet, and Nancy going to go?*

It was all over by four o'clock that day. Donald's tractor and front end loader, along with Evan's, helped load all the machinery and goods onto buyers' pickups, trucks, and trailers. Some pieces were pulled away, and Donald's tractors were driven down the road, never to work this farm again.

By evening, most of the lines of machinery were empty, with only a few remaining pieces left to be collected

Rocking Chair Moves

Later that year, Evan moved his family and belongings into the house that Donald left. The house needed fixing up first. That fall, their neighbor friends helped in the several-mile move from the farmhouse they had rented from his parents. It was a little saltbox house they had fixed up and lived in for nearly a decade. Here, Ella had carried their first child, a son who was born and then brought home to the little house on a crisp October day.

He was quite fussy, and the young wife worked hard to keep him satisfied with her own milk, comforting, and lots of rocking. Evan was not used to handling a new baby that woke numerous times each night. The morning came early too, with the cries of a hungry child. Yet all was good, with joy in the house, a sense of hope, and the newness of a family now started. Little Jamie grew fast and was soon fun to play with. Maybe that's why he was so fussy, needing near-constant feeding and attention to stimulate his soon-to-be-known inquisitive mind.

Before long, he could be found sitting on the kitchen floor opening cupboards, pulling out all the pots and pans, and stacking and organizing them as he wished while his mom prepared supper for them. My tall Evan would walk in from a long day on the farm, then pick him up with his long arms and hold him high towards the ceiling as Jamie giggled with delight.

The couple kissed as Ella peeled potatoes in the old double kitchen sink. Sometimes she would use the potato water to make homemade cinnamon rolls the next day, since it made them more moist and delicious.

Evan was glad to leave the old place and move to the new one, for his young wife hadn't been feeling well.

"I'm sure glad you're home tonight dear, I've been crying all day. I just don't know why."

"Maybe it's because I've been gone so much trying to get the other place ready. And with all the farm work, well I've probably been ignoring you."

"That sure adds to it but still that's not it. I'm just always sad."

"We'll be moving soon, so that should help you!" Evan said with a shine in his face. The old place was far out in the country and somewhat isolated.

The move was made with several pickups and a few trailers on a Saturday afternoon. Toward the end of it, they loaded a wooden rocking chair that had sat in the living room and was used to help rock little Jamie to sleep. The chair was placed in the back of a pickup truck and not tied down, since the trip would be quite short, and everyone was in a hurry for the party being held in the house following the effort. On the way, the wind rolled the chair out over the pickup tailgate, breaking it into several unfixable pieces. The neighbor friend presented it at the front door in a few trips up the four steps to the house, and offered his apologies. Forgiveness was quickly extended by Evan, since it was just a chair, and there was no need but to reassure a friend that it was all right. Internally, though, Evan paused. The chair was a bit special in its significance of a new child born, a new place, and new happiness found. *I hope this is the only thing that goes wrong here.* Ella saw the chair, then sat down on the front steps, and cried her eyes out.

The party still was good, with pizza from town and a few beers for Evan's friends, and coolers for the girls. Jamie was tired out and slept in a playpen in the living room as the gathering went on. They all talked and hoped for good things to come. The little boy was a symbol of just that. Growing in so many ways, they were. Farming and families, lives and thinking, Evan and friends were the new generation, establishing themselves as the producers of the area, helping their fathers and mothers rest a little. They were happy about the new place and the grand home they had just found a way to own. And I still wasn't even in the picture yet!

Both in everyday workload, and mentally, the older parents watched the next generation harness up to the load. It was a powerful thing. You could see in Evan along the way, the ties that develop to a farm seem to incur, in direct proportion, the creases on his face. Proud lines which are also ties - strings to never be let go. Some say it's a marriage, best not to be broken unto death. With hope, the lines softened, and the older generation hands control over. Yet, what if mistakes were made? And all was lost that was gained? That loss would bring that seemingly endless pain, like the loss of a spouse, or child, or a suicide in the family. Some say "but it's just a farm, a place for dogs to roam, kids to romp, and families to grow." That it is but there is more to it, as I began to learn soon after I arrived.

Winter came, and the first Christmas for the new family here. Evan had bought a pine tree at the local farm supply store, and set it up in the living room. He tied it to the wall with a bit of wire so the little boy could not tip it over and make a serious problem. The last ornament to be placed was the angel that sat on top. Picking up the little boy with the angel in his small hands, he reached high and let the boy set the winged ornament on top of the highest tip. Soon, the lights were plugged in as the boy squealed in delight.

Santa came on Christmas Eve, quietly, as Jamie slept in his crib upstairs. There had been milk and cookies left on the kitchen table, along with a few carrots for his reindeer. A note offered these to Santa, along with a never to be forgotten thank you for presents! Of course, the gifts were placed around the tree that night by the real Santa, as well as a note in return in bold big print with a magic marker. The first Christmas on the new farm place was pretty good.

"Honey, but why are you crying? The tree is all lit up, and our little boy is happy."

"I'm not sure. It's dark already at five pm. The days are so short. It's dreary out, and cold. I haven't got everything done for our first Christmas that I wanted to. I'm a failure as a new mother."

"Ella! But you're not! Everything is just fine. You need to cheer up."

"Sure, honey."

Over the winter, Evan continued to fix up the house. Earlier the last year, the darkened varnish of the oaken woodwork all around was taken off with harsh chemicals that melted it to be scraped away. The couple wore masks to avoid the nasty paint thinner fumes that filled the air in the rooms. But sometimes they didn't. Over time, each space was refinished. The golden oak trim work with crown molding and colonnades shone with a new luster. Similar wooden floors were all sanded and refinished as well. I know how shiny they were even in later years, after I arrived, since I could see myself when looking down in them! Accelerating quickly wasn't even possible; and not appreciated anyway! Outside was better for a good farm dog like me. There was where the risks were, for me to be on guard for. Of course this came later when I arrived.

Springtime came, and Evan got really busy on the farm. He had more acres to prepare and plant crops on. Some of the fields were miles away, so he would be gone for long hours while Ella and little boy were at home. Sometimes they would go to town to buy things and get checkups at the doctor. Ella would slip him into the car seat, strapping him in safely before she left for an outing. He expected they would be home when he got done with his work. Usually they were but lately not always. Longer days and more sun seemed to have buoyed Ella's spirits, and Evan was also happy to see her brighten with the spring light.

That night he waited for the headlights to come down the road from the east, the route they would take to get home. Yet they didn't when he thought they should. *Where are they at this time of the night? Did they go in the ditch?* When they did appear, she was quite happy though the little boy was quite tired out.

"Where were you both? I was getting really worried!"

"Oh honey, we had such a good time, and I got lots of things done until the stores closed."

"Let's just go to bed, please. I'm really tired from a long day in the field."

The next day the field work continued far away from home. Ella informed him they had not got everything done that they needed to the day before so would be leaving again.

I'm worried but I don't know why. She looks so good and is so happy, Evan kept thinking over and over as he made pass after pass in the long and wide field. Finishing after the sun went down he then drove home to find the house empty.

The minutes turned to hours as Evan waited by the door, then the upstairs window to see further.

Walking back and forth, from room to room and window to window he wondered. *Did they have an accident? Were they in a ditch? Should I start looking for them, or should I stay put at home and see them drive in finally?* He decided to wait.

It was after midnight before she called.

"We're still in the city, honey. We've got just a few more things to pick up and then get some ice cream for Jamie and then we'll be home. We've had such fun, and I'm so happy."

Jamie looked out the east upstairs window of their bedroom and could see the lights of the city far away down the river valley.

"Please come home right away, Ella! You've got to! I'm so worried about you and I've got to get up and plant tomorrow. It's going to rain next week and I've just got to get it done before the ground gets too wet."

"Okay, honey. I will for you."

She carried the sleeping boy, with sticky fingers and mouth to bed, then she and Evan both went to bed and rested.

I'm just thankful that they're safe within the home we just made. But there's something wrong with her. I've got to get her to the doctor in the morning. Oh God, make it nothing serious. Please take care of us. Please let me get this first crop planted on time. Thank you for everything. Thank you for this beautiful farm. Amen

If you were a dog and outside, you would have noticed that the lights in the bedroom did not go out as usual that night. The hallway light was on too. You would have heard the disruption upstairs, and then you would have heard it carry down to the lower rooms. Then you would have heard the little boy come down the stairs, somehow out of his crib, crying in the living room.

The next day Evan didn't plant. Instead he found himself at a doctor's office in the city, where Ella had been just a few hours before.

"She doesn't take any medications, nor abuse anything, doctor."

"It sure is a nice day out, and did you see my beautiful son? I don't know what is wrong with me but I have so much energy! Not many months ago I was so depressed, and I just didn't have any drive." "She's a beautiful person, doc. She only has goodness in her heart and spends a lot of her time taking care of others. I do know that earlier in her school days, she was very depressed for unknown reasons." *Oh God, maybe it was the fumes she had breathed too much of,* he thought.

"She had post-partum depression after having the baby, and now she has swung to into a manic state. It's like making your own drugs. Your wife has bi-polar disorder."

"Is it hard to treat? Can it be cured?" he asked.

"Yes, it is treatable, and no it can't be cured. It will take some time to figure out the right medications. You will have to stay closer to home and monitor her condition. And someone will have to care for Jamie awhile. Your wife needs to be hospitalized."

It seemed like the omen of the broken rocking chair had come into being.

The next day, Evan's father and mother came and took the little boy home with them. Evan came home around noon and didn't appear outside till that evening. He must have been sleeping. Ella did not come home for over a week. When she did, when Evan drove in with her, she came out of the car and quietly walked to the house, with her husband holding on to her.

"Where's Jamie?"

"My folks have him."

"Could you have them bring him back? I'm so sad not to have seen him for so long."

"They are on their way."

It wasn't long and the little boy toddled in, undisturbed, even though their home had been disrupted by an illness that had crept through the high hopes.

The sun was shining that day, and there were still crops to be planted. Evan's brother had come over to help get them in the ground.

Boyhood Farm Dogs

The days turned to months, and the months turned to years. All the while, there were up days and down days for Evan's wife. This seemed to reflect on the face of him,
The load seems unbearable, he thought while not sleeping well at night.

Jamie grew fast and laughed and played inside and outside. The farm grew in size, all while crops matured through the season. Evan's wife tried, and he tried, to lick the sickness that threatened the family and farm. She went to the hospital when it got bad, then came back home as soon as she could to care for her son.

Jamie got to stay during the day with grandparents, and play and "work" with his grandma in her gardens. That was all okay. Then one day his mother would come home, subdued and quiet but still the same loving person. Jamie would sit on her lap, and she would read him book after book. All the while, the time spent away and costs mounted.

Many times, when Jamie's mother was not feeling well, or was maybe gone for another stay, he would ride with his dad in the pickup truck. They would check fields and farm places. They would check irrigation systems, including the one that caused so much trouble for the previous owner, Donald.

A few months after they moved into the new place, a black dog had shown up on the back porch steps. Ella, feeling good that day, happened upon the door, and on the stoop there was a medium-sized female with big, brown, sad-looking eyes staring up at her.

"Well, hi! Who left you on our step? You must be hungry. Let me see what we have for you."

The dog looked in her eyes and swept the step with her tail. She gobbled the leftovers given to her in a tin pan, glancing left and right to make sure no one would steal her meal.

"I can tell you're a girl, so I'll call you Rosy" glancing over at an old bush of yellow roses blooming in the yard.

The dog looked up and wagged her tail even harder. Rosy it was, from then on.

Though Rosy looked hungry that day, her belly was wide and hung lower than it should. When Evan came home later that afternoon from tilling the fields, he noticed and figured the farm was adopting more than just one dog, for Rosy was pregnant and close to bearing puppies. A few weeks later, she disappeared for a day.

"Rosy didn't come to her dish this morning," she told her husband at lunchtime.

"I bet I know why!" he said with a smile.

When the dog returned, she was seen by Ella crossing the road. She fed and watered her close to the stoop by the same back door, and noticed that her center was smaller than the last time she saw her. Rosy finished, and then headed back across the gravel road. Ella decided she would follow. Near an old cedar tree, she found the dog burrowed under a dirt pile covered with a large piece of old metal. Curled around her were four puppies, all spotted white, black, and brown. Rosy gazed up and then started intently licking the pups as they nuzzled her for some nourishment.

"So, what do we have here, my lady? I see you've given us some presents!" she asked. Rosy just glanced up, while busy washing the colorful, plump little creatures.

Soon Jamie was having fun playing with the new family. In a matter of weeks, they were able to run and jump and play on him. But one day, after the pups had grown enough to follow their mother around, she took them out on a little trip, and headed down the gravel road to the west. Evan watched them scamper behind her happily. When she came home later that evening, only one pup was with her.

"Evan, the pups are lost!" she yelled towards the farm yard.

"I'll go look down the road right away," he replied.

By then the fields had grown up with crops on both sides of the ditches filled with grass. Finding anything would be hard, and a little pup would get lost easily. I sure know from my own experience! Towards evening the search was ended, after several outings up and down the little traveled roads. Neighbors were contacted as well but the three pups were never found. One male was left, so they decided they would keep him and name him Roy. He was a roly-poly kind of dog, who grew fast and was stocky. He was whiter than anything but had spots of mostly brown. His coat was medium long, and he had short ears that flopped down. Even after she weaned him, he followed his mother everywhere.

Rosy aged as the young dog grew up and matured. Her young pup turned out much larger than her. Jamie and the dogs could always be found together. They played in the woods nearby, and rode everywhere in the pickup with his dad. The dogs would ride in the back, and then reach over the side rails to catch the scent of all coming at them down the road.

The dogs, the farm, the woods, and the pickup rides all held the little boy's attention away from any worries of his mother, who still read to him, loved him, fed and clothed him. She tucked him into bed at night. When he got bigger, he chose another bedroom, so they painted it and refurnished it with warm-colored wood furniture. He slept well there most nights, yet dreamed of big things, and monsters, and grownup worries.

"Dad, I had a bad dream that woke me up."

"What was it, son? All is okay."

"I'm afraid something will happen to me, and I won't be able to take over and run the farm."

"Oh, Jamie, such a big person's worry, you don't ever have to."

"But who will then, Dad?"

I wonder if just like it's a dog's instinct to protect their owners, farm kids feel the need to protect the land they are raised on.

* * * * *

Canines grow up fast and live their lives much quicker than their human masters. We run about as soon as we walk, while we watch young people only crawl for months, and pick up the pace slowly over several years. Our speed of growth and aging causes some problems when it comes to the love between a human and their dog. Relationships develop quickly but then go all too fast in human terms. Usually we are gone first. Lucky for me, I am on dog time, and that's different. I figure it's kind of the same as people time is to people. We could go on about time and the relativity of it. Put simply, though, time is relative to perspective. My perspective is that my time here on earth is just fine, even though humans think we don't live long enough.

Roy's time on earth ended before his mother's. He liked to chase cars, and wasn't the best at it. One day a car caught him. Roads and cars sure are nice but they sure can cause lots of problems it seems.

This left a gap to fill, since Evan always liked to have two dogs on the farm. He believed that like people should have friends, dogs should too. He knew that there was a lot to learn for a new dog. Old dogs might not be able to get new tricks but they sure have a lot of knowledge to share with a young dog! So Evan began the search for a new dog to add to the family.

Evan looked in the newspaper for the next dog. I despise newspapers, especially when rolled up. A newspaper has my respect. He hung up the phone, though, lamenting that the pups were too expensive, and he never liked to jinx a new dog by paying for them. He preferred to find one that really needed a home. So he waited. Then, one day, the phone rang.

"I have four pups left, and they are getting big. I would sell one of them to you for the cost of his first shots."

"That sounds good to me. It's a deal, and I'll be over tomorrow to come take a look," Evan replied.

Rosy was going to have a new pup to train.

They were chocolate brown Labradors, and each was as cute and round as the next. The good owner was an avid sportsman who loved hunting with a dog. He was happy, at this point, to offer his pups up for someone to love and sport with. One pup seemed most interested in Evan and came up to lick his hand. That's all it took. The choice had been made. I think that Evan made a good one.

He and Ella kept the pup in the back enclosed porch for the first few nights. There was water and a food dish on newspaper laid out, along with a little box with litter in it for him. A radio played low to keep him company while they were sleeping, though it didn't quite do the trick, and he whined for a time before falling asleep. I sure know the feeling of missing my mother. Yet it passes for a pup, as the new family usually provides love to help replace the daily nurturing of a good mother dog. It was the same here, with a young boy to play with and countless new things to experience on the farm.

Hank, as they named him, grew. Maybe they named him this since that's been an eternal name for a good farmhand. Hank sure was that. The boy grew too, into a young man, who even had his own pickup truck. He was with his father when they got the little dog, and ran and played ever after.

A few years later, the boy drove that same pickup off to college. "It's a long ways away and close to the ocean", he'd said, as he patted his good friend goodbye. This left Evan and Hank to themselves. Driving down the road one day soon after, Evan watched him with a smile in the rear view mirror. The brown dog with a wide head and honest eyes, loved riding in the pickup bed. His ears would always fly back, while his eyes would open big from the wind as he reached out over the side looking forward, nosing every scent he could. Then he would wait for the tailgate to open and a call of approval for him to jump out so he could explore the new area. He wouldn't go too far, and kept his eye on the boss, while he was working on a fence or piece of machinery.

"You're either kind of missing Jamie, or liking me," Evan said as the dog came up to him and leaned against his leg. Hank looked up, panting, which looked like a smile and probably was.

"Why don't you jump in the truck and we'll go back to the house now." In a flash, Hank was in the truck with his feet on the rail ready for the wind full of scents to rush at him.

Later, if it was hot out, he might soon lie under the truck for some shade and if it was cold out, he would keep moving at his boss's side. Sometimes he wasn't allowed out, so he waited as patiently as he could for the pickup to get moving again. The days were good, and Hank matured. He grew wise and dedicated to the farm.

Hank Gets Skunked

That summer Sunday, a skunk appeared on the farm in the early afternoon. Skunks are nocturnal creatures and rarely come out for any good reason in daylight. This one came right up to the front door of the house. Hank and Rosy happened to be out by the barn dealing with a cat issue, but Hank heard his boss yell an alarm for them to come. Hank had experience with these creatures. He had been sprayed with their ghastly scent more than once. One day, he had one cornered in an irrigation pipe lying in a field, only to be hit in the face by the spray while sticking his nose into the then-obvious wrong end of the pipe. Evan stayed away from him for several days, waiting for the smell to wear off. I've been hit a few times myself and commiserate with old Hank. Trying to lick the scent off may leave the outside better, but it sure doesn't make my insides feel very good. And the taste is horrid!

Hank disregarded all his past experiences and answered his call to duty. Ella first saw the skunk at the door and shouted to her husband, who was reclining in a chair for an afternoon nap.

He jumped up and watched the skunk run back down the front steps headed for the barn. "Hank, come on over, boy, and get 'em!" he yelled.

The skunk took off from the front porch and proceeded to tour the whole farm, including the barn and pen of horses. There, right in front of his boss, he picked the skunk up, oblivious to the risks.

"Hank, no he may have rabies!" yelled Evan, only really wanting him to chase the varmint off.

Misunderstanding Evan's warning, Hank kept on and thought, *Don't worry boss, I've got it.* With the head hanging on one side of his mouth, and the tail end on the other, the brave Hank carried him off with a proud trot, understanding his duty as guardian. Hank had already squashed the critter and ended its life. He then dropped it on the lawn and calmly walked away, obeying his boss's command.

Evan scurried over to the skunk and with a shovel scooped it up, taking the risk away from the dog. *A skunk active in the day could be sick with rabies,* he thought, but tried to ignore it. Not knowing for sure what to do with the body, he placed it in the back of his pickup truck and drove off. Otherwise, he knew Hank would find the little beast again and retrieve it as a trophy of sorts.

If only I hadn't called Hank to come, thought Evan. *I never thought he would pick the skunk up and carry it off.*

After an evening of wondering about the events of the day, of why the skunk had shown up, and of what the animal might have been carrying with it, Evan went to bed but tossed and turned. He got up for a drink of water and thought of the distant spot past the reeds where he had buried the telltale black fur with a white striped tail.

"Can't you sleep, Honey?" Ella asked.

"I shouldn't have buried it. I should have taken it to the vet for inspection."

The sun rose. He had a quick cup of coffee, then jumped in his pickup and headed over to where the skunk burial happened. Again, his feet got wet as he clambered through the tall reeds that scratched his face. It didn't take long to unearth the critter and then place it in an old feed sack. The veterinarian's office was only a few miles away. After placing the bag on the ground outside the door, he went in. These places had smells I hated. Strong disinfectants over the odors of a dog kennel were only trumped by medicine scents. They all sent chills up my spine and made me pull on the leash for the exit door anytime my boss said I had to go in.

"You better have it checked, Doc."

"I'll get a sample of tissue and send it into the state lab."

"Thanks, doc."

My boss drove away wondering, *If that skunk had rabies how many of his animals did it infect?* And, at the top of his list was, *Do I have Hank's rabies vaccination up to date?*

Evan went home and started researching the disease, the risks to his animals, and the worry for his family, who would be around the dog for the next few days. They waited for the test results.

Rosy, wasn't worried. Dogs don't worry much. We live in the present, even though some of us know so much of the past. The present that day was good. I guess you could say that nice day was a gift of us living in the present.

What Evan found wasn't good. He checked a site called the Center for Disease Control, which caused him alarm.

"It says a dog that was exposed to rabies, and doesn't have a current vaccination, is a serious concern," he told Ella.

"I'm sure," she responded.

"It says it doesn't matter how friendly the animal is, it could change if the disease inflames their brain. Then they might even bite their master and infect them. Worse yet, the disease could hide in them for months, even a year, before it made a dog sick. Then when everyone thinks things are okay, the bug could jump out and bite everyone," he said.

"Well, we can't take any risks here with our family or the neighbors. Don't think you can just kennel Hank and get by. You know what you'll have to do," Ella said.

"I know."

The next morning, the kitchen phone rang. The voice on the other end was the vet's assistant, but didn't want to talk to Evan when he announced himself.

"I'll get you the doctor."

Evan knew this wasn't good.

The vet came on the line and said, "The skunk tested positive for rabies."

"I was sure afraid of that," Evan said.

"And our records show your chocolate Lab's rabies vaccination is not current."

What do you suggest, doc?"

"It's not good. You will at least have to pen him up for six months, and after that there is still a chance he could come down with it."

"That's terrible. How could I have missed the postcard you would have sent out to remind me? I'm such a fool."

"As much as I hate to say it, I would advise that you put your dog down. There is just too much risk - not only for your family but anyone that might be at your farm some day in the future."

Ella already told me what I'll have to do, he thought.

"We can't have that, doc. The farm can't afford the risk, either. I'll see you at the barn tomorrow."

Evan left, got in his pickup and put his head down on the steering wheel for a moment. He drove the short way home, got out of his truck and went over to where he had leashed Hank.

"Hey, ol' boy, he said, without nearing him. With a tear in his eye, he walked to the house to tell Ella.

* * * * *

It was a sunny morning, and the grass was green near the barn. Hank watched from his long rope at the doghouse close by, while Evan fed the livestock. He had been treating Hank really nice, though he had to be careful. He was unsure if the dog might be carrying some residue on him, so he patted him with gloves on. Hank didn't think much of it and just knew his boss loved him. Yet I bet he knew something was up, for he seldom was restrained. He never roamed, and he was getting old enough not to cause any trouble. When Evan walked by with Rosy that morning, she headed to greet Hank with a nose touch.

"Get back here Rosy", he said sternly.

The big red pickup with a white veterinarian's utility box on it came driving in and stopped close to the barn. The slim man with a kind eye got out his truck. He always wore rubber boots that could be washed off with the smelly disinfectant water he carried in the utility box. Many times he wore a smile. It was easy to see on his face that he liked dogs, and he would break into grin seeing us sometimes. Today he didn't wear one, though.

106

"Good morning, Evan."

"Good morning, doc."

The veterinarian opened a drawer in the box, pulled out a bottle, and, with a small syringe, drew a small amount into it from the smallish clear glass container. Hank was close by the white corral fence, sitting upright, obediently watching both of us. Rosie stayed close to the barn. There was a horse behind a white steel fence near them watching, with his head low in interest, peering through the bars.

"Please help me a bit," the doctor told Evan.

Evan came to Hank.

Then vet put his hand gently on Hank's big, wide head. He kneeled down and picked up one front leg.

"Please put your finger here, and hold it snug." Evan did so. The doctor inserted the very small needle into the vein just below my boss's finger and pushed on the plunger, then smoothly pulled the needle back out.

Hank sat expectantly and obediently. The veterinarian, who had been mostly trained to save animal's lives, paused.

"You can release your finger now."

With long hesitation, yet without a sound, Evan then did so. And the dog that he loved so much immediately slumped into Evan's lap. Silently, the doctor rose, turned, and, ever so quietly, walked away with his head down.

He put the syringe back in the box and did not even wash his boots. Then he opened the cab door, got in, and drove away.

Evan called his son, Jamie, later that day and explained that for another syringe, from another bottle, administered months earlier, all this could have been avoided.

There's an old saying, "One man lays it down, and another picks it up." I'm sure this goes for women and dogs, too. So I guess it could go, "One dog lays it down, and another picks up." Now, I don't think they were talking about lying down and then picking up sticks, but maybe all kinds of things, and something bigger than sticks and sleeping. Maybe it's more about life, death, and duty. I get that. There's sure a lot about all that here on this farm.

It's also about where I come into the picture.

Springtime

Early spring in Nebraska is a time when the gray and cold of winter begins to slowly melt away. There is hope in the air when a few warmer days excite those who have labored through snow, followed by muddy roads and livestock pens when it melts in March. Even the livestock look for the sun of the afternoon and lie down for a nap in it, on the wet, cold ground.

This process goes on for a few months, with fewer colder days, and then warmer ones. The grass turns green, first on the south slopes and in the road ditches. Any pasture animal searches for the few new sprigs and quickly nips them off if they can reach them through a fence line, maybe with a harvested corn field still the yellowish golden color of fall on the other side, though now graying some with decay..

Not all by chance, this spring on the farm was better in other ways too. Crop prices had risen sharply and made farming profitable. Evan and the other man who picked me up were coming back from a rare late-winter vacation in the south. They had been fishing down on the Gulf of Mexico. One of them had even splurged and paid a handsome sum for me, since he knew his daughter would love me and had wanted just my kind. I'm sure they had earned their vacation.

"Good times do not always come by accident on the farm, Ella," he would say.

I remember, years later, feeling Evan pat me on the head and say goodbye as he jumped in his pickup truck all dressed up. He first threw a suitcase in the back, which told me I wasn't going to get to go along. I figured it might be a while 'til I saw him again when this happened, so I would just keep a sharper eye on things in his absence. "I'm going to Washington, D.C. to try and solve it there, since that's where better farm prices can be legislated."

Maybe somehow he had brought those prices back to the farm, and that's why I was here, and the grass seemed to be so green - right on this side of the fence. It was lucky that things had changed, since they said costs had risen so much, and crop prices had been so low, that farming had become nearly impossible. This farm didn't need any more hard times.

First Days on a Farm

That day, I rode home in the lap of the new girl. I could see out the passenger window as we left town and headed into the countryside. Looking forward, and it being daylight and all, I relaxed and let myself sink. Maybe, too, it was the continuous hand on my fur that helped my insides feel better. It seemed the girl felt real good too, with her giggles and smile. The man driving had a kind but solid voice.

We drove by farms and fields and hills and valleys. We crossed one river over a bridge, which scared me some, since I really don't like heights!

We turned off the gravel road toward a house and barn. There were grassy areas and shady trees all around. It looked like a great place to run free and play. There were also all kinds of good places to take a poop, which was on my mind about now. It had been quite a while since last night's event. It looked like a new start, with a new girl, new place, and sun and sky all around!

Mom taught me about fresh starts. Once, when I was getting to rambunctious, she swatted me with her paw hard, leaving me to sulk for a while. I wondered if she liked me yet. In a while I went back to her, and she licked my fur, as if nothing had ever happened. Refreshed, I realized we had a new beginning, that she had forgiven me, and all I had to now for a fresh start was to forgive myself.

A large, slightly plump black dog approached the car as we neared the big old house. I lost sight of it for a moment, and I couldn't see down far enough, but I got a glimpse of the black shiny coat in the side mirror. I suspected the next move from the little girl was to open the car door, with me face to face with a big dog!

Meeting a new dog takes a few proper moves which seem to be pretty standard in dog body language. My mom taught me there is a "big dog to small dog" set of moves, and a different than "big to big" or "small to small." I have found that the latter two are about the same, since little dogs seem to think pretty "big" about themselves.

At first, I held tight to the safety of her chest. My heart beat faster, maybe to pump more blood in case there was trouble, and my nose went into overdrive. Swiftly, though, she placed me on the ground and I was left with nothing to do but stand on my own four feet. I looked at her as she stepped back, and there above me was the big black dog!

Like getting sprayed with a cold water hose, I froze.

I didn't want to send any wrong messages. I'd also figured there needed to be a time for smelling, with the big dog rightly getting the first sniff. My job was to keep an eye on it and rapidly, mechanically, turn my head so I could always see it, but freeze again as the dog smelled over me. Of course there had to be the butt smell, which is a rite of passage, and usually ends up being more of a bad whiff than a sniff. Not for me, though – being hardly being big enough to reach that high when it was my turn.

The black dog, I figured, was a Labrador. I knew from my mom that that they were pretty friendly. At my previous home, there was a neighbor black Lab who I really liked. The dog always did have its tail curled up in an attentive way. I would've done the same but since most of my tail was missing, I just pointed out what was there.

"So, you're the new pup now, huh?" said the lab.

"Guess so," I replied, thinking it a dumb statement on the lab's part, since there weren't any other pups around.

"Well, you're going to have to play by my rules."

"Ok, sure," I said, but under my breath saying, *Well for now, anyway.*

After a few rounds, our tails began to relax and heads came off the extra high position. The big dog had made its pitch for the upper hand, and I accepted. What else was I going to do? Anyway, the Lab seemed to be pretty friendly and more curious about my coming onto her farm than anything else. I didn't do much of the smelling thing except for under the leg, which immediately told me I wasn't dealing with a male. Then I heard the girl say, "Rosy."

I decided maybe it was time to play, so I ran toward the white barn with black trim, through the grassy area between buildings. The black Lab came beside me! She took the lead, and we made a few circles in the green grass that had been mowed smooth. She suddenly reached over to nip at me, and I rolled to avoid the move. It was such fun, so I jumped up and nipped at the big dog's leg, which caused her to stop, turn, and face me off. I took off running, and she chased me. Suddenly happy, we ran all over the place as the little girl and the other man looked on.

"I think they like each other!" the girl said.

"It sure looks that way," her dad replied.

This was going to be a great place, and I hoped that I could stay here forever. Yet my intuition told me that "forever" wasn't a word that was used much at this place. Suddenly, I thought about my mother and the old place. About that time, the big Lab walked by me and growled a bit.

"Just remember who the boss is around here 'til you get to know the ropes," she said.

The Prairie Girl and Lightning Storm

Eleven years had passed since Jamie was born. He was to have a late arriving sister, most surely an exciting time for him and his parents. Ella bore her with a strong effort. The little girl came to the world with a small cry and already beautiful face. Her baby scent was "like a perfume" Ella said.

The plains state of Nebraska has a history of raising some unusually strong and capable women. Girls like Willa Cather and Marie Sandoz came as early settlers of the state, and then became great authors. I'm not sure how but I suppose it was the fury of the wind, the same that made the beautiful flowing grass. It might have been something to do with the droughts that caused hunger. Or the raging blizzards that froze to death all but the strongest living things. It could have been the loneliness of the open prairie that brought on another form of hunger in their souls. The combination of all this, with the beautiful sunsets, the horses running in open pastures, and, on good days, the clear blue skies, developed something special in these women. Or might it have been their hardworking, sturdy, and wise parents that caused this?
I guess we all gotta suffer some to have a little character.

The prairie girl that I knew best was born in a more modern day. Yet her essence seemed to come from another time. It was curious, for her nature was a complicated thing, and seemed to reflect something of the past women of the wide, unsettled land.

Clara had been named after a little stream a few miles west of the farm that was called St. Claire. It was old style, yet now quite fitting for the young girl I came to know. She had a pretty face, a kindly smile, and long soft fingers that stroked my furry coat quite perfectly. When a thunderstorm threatened, she would hold me tight and whisper in my ear that it was going to be all right. It was like she knew. Then, she would set me safely in the barn on a bed of hay while I waited for it to pass. Sometimes, when it was really stormy, she would lie down with me.

On one of the first nights I sat on the front porch watching the clouds. Rosy was nowhere to be found, and I didn't understand why. The clouds swirled and there were streaks of bright light across the sky. A thunderous boom caused me to jump yet didn't hurt me, so I just kept watching. Then my hair started standing out on end, and I started hearing a buzz in the air. Suddenly I heard a startling sizzle, then a bolt of light so bright I think my hair turned blond for a second! The sound was deafening, as I saw the big cottonwood tree to the north light up more than any Christmas tree I had ever seen!

The whole thing nearly knocked me off the porch with no railing. Leaping, I cleared a bush near the foundation and sprinted for the barn. As I went through the trees, a branch came down, hitting me on the head. I veered to the left, running right into the trunk of the tree. Dazed, I yelped, then got back up on my four legs and got going again. Big chunks of ice started raining down, hitting me on the back and sides. I slipped on some of them as I chased towards the lit barn door. Making it to the hay pile in the back, I looked up and saw the horses in their stalls, watching the whole thing. They were pretty calm, given the stormy situation, but they had experience and a solid wood structure to protect them. Lucky for them, they weren't caught outside in the melee like I was.

It wasn't long before Clara came to my rescue as the storm faded and moved on to the east. I was wet, cold, and shaken from the events. It was lucky for me that I was so fast getting to the barn, or I could have been really hurt.

I'm not sure I could've outrun one of them but I would give it an even better try now after what I had just experienced.

"Oh, Ace, poor boy!" the girl said. "I'm so sorry you are upset. Didn't you hear me call, when I got the horses in the barn, to come in as well? Storms come up so quick. You must listen when I tell you something."

I'm sorry Clara, I was busy monitoring a squirrel situation and didn't hear you! That beady-eyed thing about got me killed!

She raised her brow, suggesting, "Okay, this time," as I affectionately licked her hand.

This was just one of dangers on the farm that I got myself into but the only kind I was ever frightened about. Looking into her eyes, I could always find more strength for myself.

Rosies and Posies

I quickly found my place that summer beside Rosy on the farm. She always had the lead, and I was ready to follow. *Now I know how I'm going to get along in this new territory. It's kinda like my mom taking me down the street early on.* Yet at times I thought back about my old home. *Couldn't she have kept me from leaving? I guess there probably wasn't anything she could do about it.* I bumped into the back of Rosy in my daydream.

"Keep your mind on the business," she barked.

My attention shifted to the smells coming in.

Rosy showed me the entire new place in those first months on the farm. We looked through all the sheds, including the farm shop. A few mice ran along the walls, so we gave them a good run for their money!

Near the shop was a good place to find toads too, just outside the big door at night. It seemed like they enjoyed being under the security light. Maybe they felt safer there, though it allowed us to find them. In any case, puffy, fat, gray-green toads of all sizes would end up bumping into the wall and getting trapped in corners they couldn't seem to find their way out of. It kind of seemed like punishment. *I wonder what these toads were guilty of. Or are they just not that smart?*

One evening after dark, Rosy took me to the shop, and I saw one of those toads. I was naïve and so surprised that Rosy didn't attack the first big toad we saw that night, given what an avid hunter she was. *Maybe she is being polite and wants me to have the first lick at the toad.*

"Quick, get it!" she said.

That's all it took for this new farm dog to jump into action. I sure did get a bite on the darn thing right away. It was only a second, and I had that slow moving plump, soft, kind of slimy thing in my mouth. It hardly moved, so I figured I didn't have to bite down and could save it to play with for a while.

Suddenly, though, I got the urge to drop it. Mostly, it was the horrid taste in my mouth, but, second to that, there was foam rapidly developing all around my tongue. *Has this thing been swimming in dog shampoo?* I thought. Soon I was foaming like the carwash broom at the local self-serve auto-wash bay I'd been at one time.

"Help, I'm dying!" I yelped out.

I shook my head, and white bubbles flew like the paddlewheel brush in the wash bay. Rosy just sat on her haunches and watched. *If she was a good leader, wouldn't she have told me to avoid such nasty creatures?* I guess maybe she did the right thing, since after that I dealt with toads with great care. Paw swipes only. Learning opportunities abounded everywhere, and I learned a lot, except many times it was the unsavory hard way. Sometimes, though, I wondered if I was just entertainment for Rosy. Maybe so but I think she was just getting me ready.

Leading into the Big Picture

Dogs must learn about such details as going under electrified cattle fences and keeping ears low, just like Rosy kept her tail down at critical moments. I found the places not to sleep on summer afternoons when the lawn sprinklers were on. I was educated on all kinds of critters, and usually came through encounters with them much smarter that I was before. I learned my directions back home after getting lost out in the endless rows of corn in the fields, or worse yet, in the tall soybean fields that had no rows. If I jumped high enough, I could see for a second over the plants at the peak of my leap. Clara thought it was pretty funny, seeing me bound up and down through the beans. Unlike me, she was tall and more slender, so she moved through the field with greater ease.

All in all, Rosy was a fine mentor and a fine teacher. The pattern was mostly the same during my educational outings. I would jump into the situation while she would hang back, usually in some kind of a pose, which I saw when I turned to see what she was thinking. It may be that was her mentor pose, or it could have been her humor pose, I wasn't always sure! But Rosy watched me, whether it was in the sandbur patches where I hunted mice, or the horse manure piles that I so enjoyed. In the end, I learned lots from Rosy. It wasn't long, and I was ready to take on the toughest, meanest, and downright lowest critters around the farm.

When it came time for the bigger threats, Rosy was much more serious, and gave me good advice. Then we would typically identify the problem, consider the action needed to be taken, and, with her words, "Let's get 'em!", successfully launch the attack. There were times when big problems led to difficult situations that were hard to handle. I became ready for the challenge. *Nothing's going to stop me or endanger the farm,* I thought.

I started feeling this was where I belonged.

Here I was, on an expansive farm in the middle of a large state. I had room to roam in every direction. The east and south were bordered by a road that I had to cross, which made those directions a little dangerous. So I kept my head, and watched out for threats like a speeding pickup, that would have ended my chase of something I smelled, heard, or saw across the way in the trees or field. I had heard about dogs getting run over by a vehicle, and it sure didn't sound like fun, especially since it meant a trip to the veterinarian.

Evan seemed to be on the lookout for bigger threats too. For sure, he was always worried about the growing crops, which needed sun and rain all at the right times to make them produce. That meant he had to get them planted early in the spring to capture as much light and warmth as they could in the fairly short Nebraska summers. Then he had to make sure he got them harvested and put away before the cold winter winds blew all around. A blizzard could ruin the year's effort if it locked the corn in drifts of snow.

Yet I heard Evan speak of even bigger existential threats to the farm. He was somewhat experienced in politics, and read a lot. Sometimes he would read the paper while I was lying at his feet. He would grumble and call out to Ella about something he read.

"Our government needs to make sure there is a fair marketplace for us and our neighbors, Ella."

"People can't just complain, Evan. They have to get involved."

Evan's foot stirred, and ran into my rump, causing me to lie over on my side.

"This isn't going to be good for us, Ella," he stated. "They just passed the farm bill, and they failed to set up the right policies that ensure fair prices are going to happen."

"What do you mean?" she said.

"I mean that they could have balanced the scale against the big companies we have to sell our crops to each year. They have too much control of the marketplace and keep cheating us."

"Well, what laws should have they passed?" she said.

"Legislation that would allow us to manage the supply of corn, soybeans and wheat, so that when there is too much it doesn't flood the market and depress prices. Or set up grain reserves that protect our customers when drought hits us and we just can't raise enough. That would make sure our country doesn't ever run out of food."

"That makes sense."

"It does if you're a farmer or consumer but for the big grain companies, it means they might have to pay a little more for our crops, and they don't like that," he said. "They have political clout in Washington to get their way, and they have the money and staying power in the marketplace to get their way there too. It looks like hard times may be coming, even if we do raise good crops, since the scale is weighted against us for the next four years."

Ella looked down into her lap of sewing materials and quietly said, "We'll get through it, Evan, like we always have."

"I hope so," he returned. "But it's hard to understand the injustice of it. Why does this farm always have to be at risk?"

"Well, maybe you're going to have to get involved to try and change it," she said.
"You're usually right."

Listening, I quietly righted myself on the old living room rug. I eyed the ceiling fan turning slowly and recalled the hardship stories of the past owners. There wasn't much I could do but follow his orders when he requested. And at least keep the varmints away while Evan was gone dealing with these problems.

Looks like my boss is gonna have to try and right things, I thought, *just like we try to keep things even in the barn between the cats. It takes looking out all the time.*

My eye lids closed again, and I fell into dreams of chasing things.

Rabbits in Pipe Dreams

That fall, we had another experience in smaller varmint hunting - rabbits. These gray furry creatures, with white fuzzy button tails, had a bad habit of coming onto the lawns and eating clover. Now, I don't eat clover myself but the dog in the manger didn't eat hay either. It was more that I bristled and arose when something would walk on our domain without asking. I guess, maybe, I had been born to chase them.

So we did a pretty good job of keeping the rabbits away from the yard. They always congregated in the woods across the road first. We spent a good amount of time heading them off there because we knew where they were ultimately headed. In the trees was a pile of old irrigation pipe. They were just big enough for a rabbit to hide in. We could fit our full muzzles in, but that was all. And given the forty-foot length of the pipe, this was a great place for them to safely get out of our way. But they hadn't thought hard enough.

Rosy had spent a lot of time trying to extract these long eared varmints from the pipes. She tried hard to flush them out. I could reach in further than her and was even able to bark inside the pipe. This had to be quite disconcerting for the rabbit. The problem was they usually just froze inside. Since we generally worked as a team, we stayed pretty close.

"I'll stay on this end, you get the other!' she told me.

"It's in the middle right between us!" - I could tell by how strong the scent was.

Rosy would even go to the middle of the pipe, and push it around with her nose, while my head was darn near inside the pipe.

Frustrated, she would scratch at the pipe, with no avail.

"Ouch, you're hurting my ears!" as the scratching sounds echoed in the big tube.

I'd pull my head out and bite on the end of the pipe, then drag it around. This was a bit wearing on my teeth but I didn't care - the work had to be done.

It seemed that rabbits were sort of magicians when it came to escape. Somehow, these buggers would suddenly be gone while we were busy guarding one end of the pipe. I'm pretty sure they didn't go out the other end, since we had usually had just been there...

Given the challenge of hunting rabbits in a pile of pipes, we dreamed about it a lot on lazy afternoons, after we had got done hunting them. Rosy would even act out, quivering and kicking, woofing and chasing. Sometimes I would just think about the morning we had in the woods, with the smells and sounds of leaves rustling above us. Kinda like the bigger picture on the farm, I guess. It seemed my boss and his wife enjoyed the times when they were running around trying to hold it all together.

Dreams of Better Times

Evan dreamed too, about protecting his turf that he had so much hope for. I would hear him tell Ella about his dream of better times on the farm. I was having a great time on the farm, and I think in many ways Evan and his family were as well. But there was always the worry that it would end. The worry was palpable, sometimes, when I walked beside him. It would be quiet, and he would be quiet, not asking anything of me, but I got the feeling he wanted me to be with him.

Though I must admit, when it came to suppertime, I was sure playing up to him so that he might get the idea that I was hungry. Then he would walk toward the barn where my dinner dish was, and fill it from the sack of dog food kept there. If I did a little dance, he might give me a little more, which made me even happier! My hope was suddenly turned to reality. Hopes and dreams.

Dreams are where good things start, I think. And I believe this is where Evan started, as he began to conceive a plan to ensure farmers like him wouldn't have to worry so much about the price of corn or soybeans. He knew this was possible, since he had heard his father talk about times when things were better, more stable, and more profitable.

When he had bought the farm that I lived on, times were really bad. The odd thing was that it was hard times that gave him the opportunity to buy it. Yet the reason he had the chance, and the unfairness of it for the previous owner, nagged on him. They say it's a dog-eat-dog world, a term which makes me feel sick, since I never want to be that kind of canine. But I get the idea that you have to be tough and take advantage of opportunities when they arise. Like when a rabbit finally jumps out of a pipe. Evan thought things should be fairer, though, and I could see by the look on his face, when he spoke of the former owner, that he was sad.

Soon, I started seeing Evan leave the house early in the evening. He would return hours later, and seemed tired but satisfied.

"We had a good meeting tonight, Ella."

"Did you pass on my idea about trying to get some sort of support price for corn passed?"

"Yes I did, and they liked the thought. There were quite a few other farmers there, and a speaker who educated them about possibilities that would make farming work out better."

"We'd better all do something, or we're not going to be able to pay our farm loan at the bank," Said Ella.

"You don't have to tell me that," Evan replied, sounding a bit short I thought.

Sitting there, I wondered, *What would happen to me then? Would I get to stay on the farm? I sure don't want to leave this place. It's the place of my dreams.*

It wasn't long, and I saw him with a paper in his hand when he left, thanking Ella for helping him with his speech. Well, I didn't think he had anything wrong with how he spoke. I longingly watched him drive down the lane, wishing he would take me with him. Then I would know more about what he was up to, and what his speech was all about.

'Coons and Cottonwoods

Nebraska is known for a majestic big tree called a cottonwood. When I walk up to one, it takes me quite a few steps to get around it. And when I look up, I get dizzy some, seeing the sky through the huge tree branches. The only troubling thing about the tree is that in late May it would shed "cotton" that floated in the air everywhere. Sometimes it would get sucked into my nose, causing a big sneeze.

There are several cottonwoods on the farm here that were planted many years ago by Jessie, the first farm owner. I love to hang around them since they are a great place to find varmints of various types. Squirrels seem to like them, building nests high in the boughs where not even a cat ventures and certainly not me. Some good coonhounds are known to climb trees, though. I prefer to deal with pests on the ground, mostly. But there have been exceptions to this.

One day I encountered an intruder lurking by one of these trees, while I hung around a hired hand as he built a new fence. Since these trees get to a hundred years old and get so wide, they have a habit of rotting from the inside. Many times they become hollow in the center. I walked by the hole in this one. *What's that smell?* And I knew in an instant it was the pungent scent of a raccoon. I stuck my nose and head into the hole, and peered up. All I saw was darkness but I knew from the snarl that I had hit pay dirt. I had it cornered in this tree since no daylight also meant no escape-hole at the top. *I've gotta go in and defend the farm from this varmint.*

The opening was just a bit bigger than me, so I was able to claw my way in, and found I could wiggle my way up the hole to access this formidable opponent. I figured the only way to deal with this critter was to drag it out and fight it on my own turf. So I kept crawling until my nose ran into some coarse, smelly fur. It was trying to escape me by climbing up, so I grabbed onto his rump and went into reverse gear. Given my strength, and gravity advantage, we started moving down the inside of the tree.

"Let go of me, you stubborn dog. This is my hole!" it snarled.

"Not a chance!" I mumbled through a mouthful of fur. The snarling only got louder as we struggled down the hole. When I got the varmint to the bottom, though, I realized the hole was stopped up by a chunk of punk wood. My plan was about to get plugged up! Luckily, the hand heard the commotion, and soon I felt a boot at *my* rump, as he kicked at the chunk of punk. That was all it took, and in one swift move, I yanked myself and my adversary out, with the furry pest tightly gripped in my teeth!

I knew when we reached the open air, there would be quite a fight. It was time for a team effort, and as usual my sidekick Rosy was there waiting for the ensuing battle. That critter never had a chance as we circled and lunged from two points. But it wasn't long before got away and high-tailed it out of there, across the cornfield, as fast as it could run.

"I'll be back! That's my house!" it snarled.

"A house made of sticks!" I quipped.

We looked at each other, and by the face of Rosy, I knew she had decided to let it go.

None the worse for wear, I gathered myself, rested a bit, and then made the hike back to the barn with my sidekick close by. It was time for a drink of water at the watering trough. I then gave myself a good bath in the sun by the doghouse. Evan stopped by after the battle and gave me a pat on the head.

"Pretty good moves you put on there, I hear, Ace. I didn't know you were a climbing dog!" he said.

All in a day's work, I returned, with a few easy pants, looking up beaming.

Rolling over, I positioned myself for my favorite, a belly scratch, and got it.

I sprawled out there that afternoon in the now-waning sun on a crisp fall day, here on the farm. All was well, and, most importantly, all was under control—at least on my end.

Flushing the "No-Gooders" Out

My experience told me where to find varmints. Following scent trails, and then smelling up a hole at the base of a big tree would be a good example. Most likely, something was going to be hiding there. Evan, in his search for a solution to the plight of farmers, started figuring this out too. He knew someone was spoiling the pie, so he educated himself to learn who and what it was. Sometimes he found out that it was simply those who had a different interest than he did.

I'm not talking about things such as hunting or fishing or something. But an interest in what seemed best for them, and what made them profit for a better life. Most times, it was all about money. Many times this came at the expense of others. That's where my boss really drew the line, since here is where some of the worse human qualities lay, he thought.

"They call it greed, Ella," he said while reading the paper at night in his chair.

I'd squirm a little, having certainly been accused of greediness by my feline associates at the scrap dish, *though they're sure calling the kettle black I thought.* Those darn cats were always selfish between themselves! And never once offered me a piece of meat or even a little crust of bread! Instead, they would run off with it and hide 'til they had eaten it all.

My boss went clear to Washington, D.C. several times. One time he took me with him in his car. That's where we heard the big speech on the steps of the Lincoln Memorial. He told me about Lincoln- said that man was all about fairness and honesty. *From the looks of his statue sitting in a chair, that sure was a big man,* I thought.

We heard a man make a speech in front of a big crowd of farmers. The man used farmer terms and said, "Boys, the creek water won't clear up until you get the hogs out!"

When I heard this, I stiffened up a little, thinking there was something I was going to have to chase. He must have felt it through the leash he kept me on.

"There's no chasing to do, Ace, just laws to change, in a respectful way," he said under his breath, as he listened intently.

That made sense to me, and I understood it to mean that there had to be fences and rules that made things fair. Hogs shouldn't be in a creek which people might need. And maybe even farmers shouldn't be allowed to charge too much for their crops when supplies were tight, either. I was starting to get it. Looking out over the pond of water, I wondered if the farmers were in the same position I was in then; kinda kept on a long rope.

We came home after days on the road, where I saw lots. He told the neighbors that we had seen great rallies of farmers all wanting the same thing; a fair price for what they produced.

"This would only come through a fair marketplace that provides enough for everyone," he told the neighbor to the west. "We're supporting proposed farm bill legislation that would help".

"That won't work. It's been tried before," he replied.

I growled softy.

"Ace, be quiet!" he said.

Yet, I saw Evan's mouth curl up and his eyebrows rise when he spoke of the possibility. He said they'd "walked the halls of Congress in peace, talking to every office we could," and I took that to mean there were long buildings with hallways to offices of senators and congressman who I bet he wanted to speak with. My head slumped in between my front paws when I thought about him walking all those halls alone. I sure wish he would have put me on a leash to be there with him, to protect him. Instead he would leave me in the hotel room.

"You can't go with me to the Capitol, Ace. It's a sacred place for our nation."

Well, I'd be respectful, my tail wagging, as I looked up at him hopefully.

I never saw any gatherings around home like that. But, when my boss started figuring out who was "eating his lunch" as he called it, he got pretty upset. Then he decided it was only right that he should stand up for injustice and speak out. If that meant being in a peaceful crowd of farmers at the steps of the

Capitol Building or the Lincoln Memorial, I guess he figured that was what he should do.

One day when we were walking by the U.S. Capitol steps with a small group of fellow farmers, we saw an unusual and a slightly disheveled-looking man, walking up the slope to the building, with one boot off and another one on. He was kicking the boot up the hill, mumbling complicated words. When he got to the farmers, he asked what they were doing. Of course, my boss wondered what *he* was doing.

Being polite, Evan said, "We're here in Washington since we figured out who the trouble-makers are. We're trying to tell Congress how to keep the foxes out of the hen house, so to speak."

The man seemed to get it from the inspired look on his face, and quickly said, "Oh! You farmers want parity, not charity!" and walked away, kicking his boot on up to the steps.

"Yes, parity, equality and fairness. This is what our government is all about," my boss said.

As for the shoe, well, I sure could have carried it for him, or dragged it by the shoelaces. But my master tugged on the leash a little, as the man left, still kicking his shoe up the hill.

"He's not very well, Ace. Just let him be. Though he sure has some things right and something to offer, even in his sickness. I sure appreciate him."

Seems to me the world is a pull of strings between equality and inequality, fairness and unfairness, sickness and health. *It's kinda gray at times too. It seems to be kind of a tug of war all the time. I guess we'll always have something to chase, even if it's just our own boot.*

Squirrel Tales

I guess it could make their squirreldom stronger as a group - you know, us chasing them at all hours, and catching at least the weakest. Survival of the fittest, I suppose. But what happens if we dogs make them extinct? Squirrels seem to underestimate our abilities as hunters.

From Evan's front porch, where we sit with him in the morning as he drank his coffee, we could see the lane to the road. Across the road was a sort of forest of trees. Beyond that was a corn field, where the dried mature grain made perfect food for a squirrel. Along the short lane was a row of trees on each side. They were close enough together that the branches almost met, but not quite. Near was a huge tree, between the forest and the lane. All these trees seemed to be a magnet for squirrels. One would think that the forest is enough, given the hundreds of trees there, but I figured there must not be enough danger there for these creatures. About twice a week, a squirrel would cross the road in the daylight and enter our domain. My internal clock almost tells me when it's about time to happen. I wonder if they don't have one too, and decide it was risk-on time again! We all knew the dividing line between our turfs. The road was also about as far as us dogs could see, though our smellers smelled for us well beyond that. That's if the wind was right.

That winter morning, a squirrel again strayed onto our side.

My sidekick happened to notice it first, as I was looking the other way—of course, scanning for other varmints.

With my classic quick, sharp twist of my head, my eyes narrowed in on the critter. *I think you need some counseling as a species,* I thought. I heard scratching, scrambling paws on the tile floor of the porch, so I made the same sound and leaped off through the front bushes. No seconds were spared. Rosy ran just a few paces ahead of me on the lawn, and looked back.

"Are you coming?" she said.

She had slowed just a bit to look back at me full speed behind her. There was nothing else I could do but run smack into her silly black rump. We both rolled a few times, yet somehow ended feet down, scrambling to continue the chase. Turf chunks flew. This error gave the vermin just enough lead to climb the middle tree in the row, as we bounded to the trunk of the tree. I almost got the squirrel's tail in my mouth.

"Lucky, squirrel!" I barked.

The squirrel climbed to the top of the tree, since it probably wised-up and feared for its fur. Smart creature, I must admit. There it sat.

"Come on up, the breeze is nice up here," it chattered. "I saw that collision, you couple of bumbling fools."

"The real bumble is on you!" I replied. "You're sure lucky we hit, since your hide isn't tough enough to protect you from my teeth!" *Though they're not as sharp as they used to be,* I thought.

"You're lucky you didn't try, since my superior squirrel teeth woulda cut right through those thin lips of yours!" the overgrown chipmunk replied.

"Fat chance!" I said, regretting my choice of words, since I could feel the fat lip that would have caused. The varmint continued to chide us, like we were in the wrong and should leave the premises.

"Just relax and take a break. We got this under control," Rosy said.

I lay down and readied for an extended watch. Experience told me that we had more patience than our opponent. Morning came and went. We moved positions from time to time, to keep an eye on the jumpy animal that kept on taunting us just because we couldn't climb the tree. It didn't seem to understand how many other abilities we have as dogs, aside from this one. After lunch—we hoped for squirrel—it was our typical naptime. But not today; there was work to do.

Myself, I can keep an eagle eye on my prey for hours on end. Usually. This time I think I was lulled to sleep by the murmuring of Rosy as she dreamed.

"Rosy, wake up! Show time could be anytime," I said.

"I was just closing my eyes for a second,"

Both of us could have also been a bit tired from being on guard duty a good part of the night. My lids dropped only for a moment in a power nap. Of course, the squirrel, in its great angst to escape our jaws, caught sight of this and made a break.

It must've jumped from about twenty-five feet up from the last time I saw it, and hit the ground with a thump between the trees. I leapt up and was on him quick like.

"Escapee!" I barked to Rosy.

"On it!" Rosy barked back, as she leaped up.

But it made it to the tree just ahead of me. This scene repeated itself through the afternoon until the squirrel had made it to the last tree on the lane. I think we were a bit sharper now too. My sidekick sure should've been, given all the naps she squeezed in.

About that time, Clara, who was a teenager now, walked down the gravel lane leading a horse back to the barn. It was her favorite horse - the one that she had grown up with. This worried the squirrel, which leaped from the tree, with us awake, and it with no tree even close!

"You don't have to worry about her but now you better worry about us!" I barked this time.

We were on it in a flash! Of course, I got to it first, and grabbed it by the scruff of its furry neck. Rosy grabbed the tail. We didn't have a plan about who was to carry off the critter and deal with it, since it would only take one of us. There was a short struggle.

It was kind of like watching two kids go for a fly ball, as I had seen in town at the kid's games. Sometimes it gets dropped. Not in this case, though. We'd both latched on good. The squirrel seemed to get longer as we both tugged backward. Growling and digging in for traction, I could hear the squirrel's angry voice get higher!

"Let go! Only one of you hounds at a time!" it chirped.

About then, I heard another sound, an even higher pitch. It was the telltale scraping of a fork in the backyard of the house. This was the typical dinner bell for us, and it meant the scraps were coming outside. It was usually a race to keep the cats away from the luscious treats prepared and left over just for us. Double duty had arrived, which happened often on the farm.

Lucky, it only took one of us to deal with this little varmint. Instead of wasting our energy on both ends of the squirrel, Rosy dropped the tail and headed for the other situation. This left me with a furry body wrapped around my nose and claws digging in my cheeks. But it wasn't long before it hightailed out of there, across the cornfield, as fast as it could run.

By the time I got to the scrap bowl, my sidekick was already back on the porch after what smelled like a meal of bacon grease on burnt toast. I would have hoped for my share but that doesn't seem to be a dog habit, leaving anything for anyone else! We both wound up licking our paws on the front porch. Another nap was in order before the nightly watch. All was well from my present vantage point on the farm. Thinking about the critter getting away from us, *I sure wouldn't want this farm to get away from us,* as I fell into a sleep.

Short Crops, Market Tops

The summer before had been awful dry. I remember the grass was quite brown already in the spring. The wind had been blowing a lot, and this seemed to just make things get dryer even faster. Evan had got the crops planted earlier than usual, since there were few rains to slow him down in the fields. There was enough moisture to get it to grow all right, and things started out pretty good.

The grain markets, though, had not. After several years of good crops, there were ample supplies of corn and soybeans left over from the last harvest. This made the grain buyers lackluster in their willingness to bid up for my boss's crop. He called the Big Grain Company one day, to try and sell them some.

"Hi, what's your bid on corn today?" he asked the grain buyer.

"We're bidding three dollars a bushel. The market is up at the moment - three more cents. They're calling for rain this weekend. If that happens, this price won't last long," he said.

"Seems to me, the forecasters haven't been right lately so I think I'll wait. It's awful dry across the corn-belt. If it continues, we're sure going to eat up our extra supply of grain quickly."

"It's your call," replied the buyer. "I'm here when you're ready. There seems to be a lot of corn to come in before harvest. Farmers got to get their bins emptied."

I know he's right, and he's got me, Evan thought but didn't say, as he hit end on his cell phone.

Then as summer rolled around, the weather people quit talking about rain and started talking about heat. Soon Evan was irrigating the fields as much as he could. It didn't rain that next weekend after the call, and the market shot up. My boss knew he had plenty of last year's crop to move yet, and could even start forward selling some of what he might grow this year—though he really didn't know how much he might produce, given the weather. Watering crops sure did help give him hope he would raise some.

All the time, the grain market kept rising. And rising. Soon the cash price for corn was a dollar higher than what he had been offered late in the spring. It seemed, though, that the market could even climb another dollar per bushel. My boss had plenty of loans to pay and some losses to recover from the previous years, when the prices were too low to allow him to break even. So, though he had plenty to sell due to a good crop season, he held on.

"I've got to make it good this time, and catch this market at its highest," he told Ella one day.

"I know, honey. You've worked so hard for what's been raised. Maybe now we can cash in some on a good market price, and make some money and pay off some loans," she replied.

"Yup, we'd better hang on a little, though. The market forecasters are saying this thing is going higher, just like the weathermen are saying this year is getting drier," he said, chuckling on his little rhyme.

"But Evan, it's a profitable price right now."

"This year could end our worries!" he said.

That Friday, the grain futures market was up hard. The weather report said there was only a slight chance for rain over the Midwest the next week, and then Evan understood the seriousness of the situation. Grain traders were banking on a short crop year and speculated what was about to happen. That Monday it rained. And it rained Tuesday, and Wednesday.

Like trying to catch a falling star shining in the night, Evan tried to grasp what was happening. It seemed like the grain traders knew more than he did, and it was probably the case. They had the best insight, with teams of experts watching nearly everything affecting the market simultaneously. Suddenly, it seemed the crop was saved across the grain belt of the country. Like magic, the weather had changed.

"Honey, there's two inches in the rain gauge this morning. It's really going to help the crop here," he said. "The grain markets open at 9:15 a.m." as he looked up at the clock. "I better call soon and see what they're bidding." He paced back and forth.

"Hello, yes, the market hasn't opened yet, but they're calling for it to be limit down today, which is thirty cents, and we're taking protection of another twenty, so that's the situation," the buyer announced. "I've got lots of farmers calling me this morning wanting to sell me corn right now, so I better let you go."

Evan got off the phone and paced even more. I saw him go to the computer, where he could read the news and market reports, and study them intently. I saw him go in the other room and heard a thud on the wall between us. He came back in and read some more, as the market opened and the numbers scrolled across the screen, with an arrow down by each one. The arrows were on all the lines, clear across the screen. I could see that, and I saw my boss's head tip down towards the floor as well.

Quietly, I approached him and leaned up against his leg. It was all I could do. Evan reached down and stroked the top of my head and put my ear between his fingers and rubbed softly.

"This is a disaster. We've lost all our profits for this year and next, all in three days."

No one was there for him but me.

"How do I break this to Ella when she comes home from the store?"

I thumped my tail on the floor and looked up at him.

Ten days later, I heard my boss make another call to the buyer. They seemed to be the only game in town at that time, with the best bid.

"We're only paying two thirty-five today."

"What are your people saying, do they think there'll be any recovery?" he asked the buyer.

"They don't see it going up much, now that the weather has changed. And acres are up this year too."

"Two forty and you've got a deal," as he thought, *I guess I better take it. In two months my bins need to be empty, since harvest will be here, and I need the room.*

"We can do two thirty six and that's all.

He paused, the said "Ok, I accept"

"I'll send out the contract for you to sign," the buyer for the Big Grain Company replied.

As I walked into the other room, I noticed the boot-toe-sized hole, low in the wall, that hadn't been there earlier this spring. *He's worried about the farm again,* as I watched him sit at his desk piled with envelopes and papers; "bills" he called them.

Cats, Scraps, and Scrappy Cats

Usually, late mornings on the farm were made up of washing and drying my fur after a romp on dew-covered grass, or the wet snow in the winter. The sun was just the right strength for this about then, on the east or south side of the house and barn. I could also multitask by doing lookout for incoming cars and trucks to the farm shop. If so, there were announcements to make and wheels to check. Or we were making sure the cats were staying in line as they crossed from the house yard to the barn. They needed constant attention, since they liked to sneak food from my dish when I wasn't looking. They also seemed to get in fights from time to time, and then I had to play sheriff. It only took a few barks and threatening snaps to get them to settle down and play nice, most times.

I had come to terms with farm cats. You noticed I added "farm" before "cats," since they are a different breed. I did have some early experiences with city cats when I was very young, so I understood the difference.

Farm cats were a tougher lot to deal with, yet me and my sidekicks always had the upper hand. I can't call them varmints, but they are a close second. About all they do is help us catch mice in the place. The thing about farm cats is they are pretty scrappy. They had to learn to barn fight early on in life. I think some of it comes naturally; already bred into them I should say.

In extreme cases, though, like when a neighboring scruffy tomcat tried sneaking into the barn, I would have to really launch into full alert. This left the cat looking like it stuck its tail in a wall outlet, scrambling to ditch the barn. Or, if he was underhanded and a scaredy-cat, he would run up the barn stairs to the loft and wait for me to get tired of waiting for him to come down. I figured this long spell for him in a hot hayloft all day was a good trespassing penalty.

Pretty much each spring, the neighbor's sly, low-down black tomcat, who was missing part of an ear, and looked at you with eyes half shut, showed up for a few days. Things got pretty unsettled when he did, and there were usually a few fights with the farm's own head male cat. We had to try and police the situation, and be on call day and night during this time. There's only about so much we could do though. When we saw him, the alarm went out, and we headed off in full chase mode. One night Evan saw another tough-looking, scroungy, yellow-striped one in the barn while he was feeding us. I'm not quite sure how I missed him, but maybe it was the clatter of dog food hitting my dish that distracted me.

As soon as I was aware of the situation, I leaped from my dish on the big wooden box where I usually eat. I sprang into action. He ran to the far end of the barn. When I reached the yellow-bellied intruder, the fight was on. He knew it, so I had to do my best to drag him from the junk-filled back corner he was trying to escape to. Things were crashing down, and quite a ruckus was developing, but my mission was clear - evict this menacing tomcat. All the other felines kept their heads down and ears pinned back, not moving a bit. I'm sure they felt a bit confused with him being a cat, too, and me being a dog that, at times, would chase them. But this situation made for an unusual alliance, since they didn't seem to like a stranger eating out of their dish either!

There were soon claws on my back, though it wasn't long, and I had the upper hand. The fur flew, and you'd swear a panther was screaming in the barn.

I made my own noise to counter. Barking and growling, I said, "Get your crooked tail out of here, you low-down intruder!"

"Not without a fight!", as he took a swipe at my nose.

Luckily, I dodged that one and charged just after the paw swooped by. Biting down on his scruffy neck, I tried to carry him out of the arena. Other cats all around were watching the drama play out, some sitting up on bales of hay and others on perches in the horse stall windows. I felt kinda like I was in a tiger pit, with all the spectators watching from their balcony seats. He countered by curling up and clawing me with his back feet. I threw him up in the air and let him fall. When he hit, I was on him again, pouncing like he was a mouse. A tiger sprang back at me, though, so I backed up in retreat to figure out my next move. *This is a tough one,* I thought. He headed for another corner. Then I had him. There, I swiftly roughed him up, before I let him escape, and he headed out the big barn door.

The other cats started thawing their freeze stance and began slowly moving again, slinking away.

"Nice job, Ace," the grey striped one said.

"Yeah, all in a day's work- hope you learned something," I replied shaking the fur out of my mouth.

I figure they thought one of them might be next, given what they had just witnessed. But I had showed them all, and done what Evan wished: evicted an intruder. I marched back to my perch by my dish.

"You're just lucky it wasn't you," I told them.

"That's worse than what I get into when I visit the neighbors farm," the farm's fluffy haired gray cat said.

My lips curled up a little as I looked at him, but I didn't say anything and headed to over to my boss. Evan picked up the debris without saying a thing other than, "Good dog."

You bet, boss. I'm proud to have been able to help.

It's nice to have an audience when things go well, and you accomplish a service for the farm. But sometimes the crowd gets a little big. The thing about farm cat populations is they seem to be like a snowball rolling down a hill that got bigger all the time. One year, there were only a few in the barn but, before you knew it, there were twelve. Then the next year, there were twenty. I don't know how Evan could feed them all, but figured I would'a had more to eat if there weren't so many to fend off when they hit the scrap bowl. It got discouraging when you're just trying to live a peaceful dog's life on the farm. This all seemed to have something to do with the neighbor's tomcat, showing up. That's why it was in my interest to "take care" of him.

When the back door of the house opened in the evening, before I heard the resonating scrape of a fork on a plate, I *always* dropped what I was doing. Sure, that may have been resting and readying for the next situation. I didn't have to run there like the cats did, since I could usually clear them out after the door banged again. Then it was my turn at the dish, even though the more minor species of the farm had gulped down a bite or two.

"Ok, move on out, I'm here," I said, with a low head and sideways glare.

"Sure, no problem," the calico mother cat would say in a mumbled voice, since her mouth was packed as full as she could get it, after swallowing the first bite without even a chew.

"I'll just take this one piece and run to the bushes, no problem," the gray striped would grumble, as he lifted the steak bone high to clear the ground.

"Wait a minute!" I said. "That's my bone!"

He dropped it, readied to be rolled, and ran before I taught him a lesson.

Evan watched me deal with the situation at the dish one day.

"Ace, farmers are just like you. We always have to fight for scraps they throw us in the marketplace, while everyone further up the food chain gets a heaped serving of money."

I just gulped down the last bite and licked the bowl a little.

"It's time I figure out the system, and get going, or I'll be forever picking up the remains of what they give me for what I produce."

Well, it's gonna be awful hard, I thought as I looked up at him, and swept the sides of my mouth with a tongue to get the last bit.

Secret Midnight Meetings

I would overhear some of the stories my boss told about his travels to the big city of Washington, D.C.

"We seldom get a fair price," he told the congressman. "We work a year to produce a crop, with all the planning it takes, machinery to fix and prepare, field work to do, and then planting of the crops themselves," he went on.

"We only receive a few cents out of what a box of corn flakes or a gallon of milk sells for," he complained.

"We usually receive just enough to make it to the next year, and then do it all over again." I can attest that there was the weed control, the irrigating to do, and then there was the harvest. After harvest, then came the storing, marketing, and hauling of the grain. And then all the paperwork, and business.

"Well, what do you think I can do about it?" he replied.

"You know the farm program is about balancing the scales between buyer and seller," Evan said.

"I understand, and sure would help if I could, but there are other folks in the food chain that don't want us meddling with the market," he said.

"Well, I know when somethings broke, and on the farm I make sure I fix it," Evan said.

"It's not always that clear in Washington, though most of us mean well and are determined to do so," the congressman said.

This was probably true. I heard my boss tell a story one day to a neighbor. He had been told it by a man who was there, who a few years later became friends with my boss. It was about a midnight meeting in a senator's office on Capitol Hill. It was kind of a secret meeting, and Evan sure wasn't invited. The senator who held it was the chairman on the powerful Agriculture Committee. Negotiations had come to a head on the farm bill that was being debated in Congress. My boss was in town again, representing farmers by talking to as many people who would listen to his concerns.

A few people of the highest authority had met late that night to agree between themselves the path forward. It was supposed to be a fair thing, with even a farm corn group representative present. The secretary of agriculture for our nation was there, along with his top assistant.

They were deciding what they could agree on for the support prices for corn, a principal crop of our country.

"Let's drop the support prices one third, and then we'll sure export more of this glut to other countries," the Secretary said.

"Do you think that will work?" said the Senator from Kansas.

"The big grain companies do," said the Secretary.

"What about you, do you think your corn organization members would support this move?" asked the Senator.

"I think so. But just one minute. I'll have to make a phone call to make sure," he replied.

The others watched him reach for a phone on the other side of the room. There was some quiet discussion, which the assistant to the secretary of agriculture could barely hear.

"Yes, sir, I'm sorry to bother you at such a late hour, but this is important," he said.
"These numbers are quite low, but I know your wishes so I thought you would want to hear," he continued.

"Yes, yes, I understand, sir. We appreciate the huge financial support you have given our organization over the years. I will tell the senator that these prices for corn will be acceptable to our organization."

He placed the phone down quietly on the handset by the plush leather couch of the senator's office. The assistant looked away as the person walked back across the room.
"Gentleman, those numbers are acceptable to our organization," the representative replied.

"Well, then, this meeting is over, and thank you, gentlemen, for your cooperation," the senator said.

The young assistant to the secretary slid in alongside him in the black limousine that picked them up. The streets by the capitol were quiet, and dimly lit by old ornate street lights.

"Mr. Secretary, that wasn't fair, what happened just now."

"Oh, but that's just the way it is sometimes, my friend," he replied.

The assistant sat in the luxury of the car and thought to himself, *I'll never be a part of something like this again.*

Evan came home after that, I remember. He told a neighbor that the farm bill had passed through Congress the next week, and the president had signed it. That fall corn prices dropped by one-third and stayed there for the five years that the bill covered. I recall seeing the look of disgust on my boss's face as he looked at the market screen day after day, week after week. The pacing he did afterward, with his hands behind his back, sure told the story for me. I also wondered. I was afraid for what would become of the farm. It sure felt like we were going to lose it. I figured Evan felt like me in the tree with the raccoon, but the hole didn't get cleared by someone, so he was trapped.

Later that fall, I remember seeing my boss going to the mailbox every day, after the carrier had stopped. It was a bit unusual, since Ella did it most of the time. He would walk back to the house and step in for lunch, or dinner, as they called it on the farm. Supper was the evening meal.

"Did it show up today?" she quietly asked.

"No, not yet" he replied.

"Do you think it will be enough to cover the difference and pay off the loan at the bank?"

"I hope so. My banker has been fair, and he needs to get paid."

"Maybe it will come tomorrow."

The yellow formal envelope, from our government, with a check inside came the next week. I could tell, since Evan's feet moved quicker as he walked to the house with the mail in one hand and the envelope in the other.

"I didn't want to take a check from the taxpayers to make ends meet this year," he told Ella.

"You know we have no choice, though, don't you?" she said.

"I do, and I hope it's enough."

Late that night, my boss was still up. I was lying on the floor close to the corn stove, which made the room warm and inviting. A soft glow from the flame at the window lit the room some. My boss had reached in the top cabinet and pulled out a bottle. He poured himself a drink of some brown liquid that I smelled in the air but wanted no taste of.

"We raised a great crop, and we got it harvested and put away. I don't know what more they want. It is food, and we've got to have plenty for everyone, including those who don't have the land or rainfall to do so in other countries," he said to Ella. "Now, when the bins are full, and our country is fed, they say it's not worth anything, because there's too much!" His voice got louder, and his back stiffened. He poured the contents of the short glass down his throat. "It's really gold, that's what it is! Golden corn: the basis for all kinds of food in our pantries."

Ella looked down, as she stood at the kitchen table with her hand on a chair. She reached over and placed her hand on his.

"I'm so sorry, Evan, but you know there's always next year."

I got up and went to his other side, and pushed my nose into the palm of his other hand.

"I'll be okay, you two. Please just let me sit for a while and figure this out. Ella, could you pour me a little more before you leave?"

I didn't want to go, so lay down quietly, hoping he wouldn't notice I was still there.

"You're okay, Ace," he said.

My tail wagged, and I sighed a little, before I went to sleep.

Snakes Do Offer Breaks

As my boss found out in business, snakes in the grass can be a problem. They were also a common problem around the house yard for several years. It was good we were close by when they appeared. Jamie, as a teenager, typically mowed the big lawn about the time of day we were napping. We hoped that they would stay away from where we were sleeping, so we didn't have to be bothered and move.

But the mower sometimes stirred up a nasty one. Mostly of the smaller kind, though once in a while Jamie ran into a big bull snake. That spring day, he intercepted one of these on the house lawn, which had probably just come out of hibernation. He gave a quick shout to us, "Get 'em! It's a snake!"

We sprang into action, knowing what we were probably up against before we even got there. Sure enough, there was the big, brown, thick snake with diamond-like marks, all coiled up in the road ditch by the house yard. They like to mimic a rattler and even sound a bit like one, so I'm very careful to not get bit just in case. This one was coiled up, but I guess as long as Rosy from head to tail.

Snakes are quick and agile. Rosy was ready, having been all rested up and everything. She would jump in and snap at the snake, but it would strike back with lightning speed. Rosy worked in a round and round action, trying to find a way to its

163

tail, which always seemed to be a safer bet than going for its head. This snake, though, was good at staying on top of it, twisting and writhing to always be facing her.

It became clear more assistance was needed. With caution I approached, keeping my front feet ready to jump. I hesitated, with my head low and back arched up, ready for anything. There's a little voice in my head that keeps telling me, "Watch out, you're dealing with a snake!"

In this case, though, and at my boss's strong encouragement, I had to help out. Waiting for the snake to be facing my sidekick, I would enter at the rear of the fight, guerrilla warfare-style, and strike when the snake wasn't looking at me. This strategy soon looked like it would work, since the snake just couldn't guard both front and back at the same time. After a few tries I got a break and successfully grabbed the snake's tail. With a quick flip of my head, while leaping a bit, I threw the snake clear across the road into the tall grass. I'm sure he couldn't slither away quickly enough.

It was lucky I stepped in, since Rosy seemed quite worn out. There was lots of slobber around her mouth, and her tongue was hanging out, dripping fast. I'm sure she was heading for the water tank to recharge her cooling supply.

Evan seemed quite satisfied with me as he walked back across the lawn to the farm shop.

"Looks like it takes more than one to nail down a snake," Evan said as he looked down at me. I strutted along with him, head held high. I wonder if he was thinking about the wrongdoers in Washington, and I was glad that at least we could deal with those types here.

Fields and More Fields

"Well, if we can't get much for our crops, then I guess we'll just have to raise more," my boss told Ella one morning. "There's a farm a few miles from here that is for rent, so I put a call into the owner to see what he's asking per year."

"Do you think you'll get it rented?" she asked.

"I hope so. It's a pretty good farm, and our machinery size can handle some more acres, I think. We're just going to have to cut our costs and get more efficient, if we're going to make it."

Listening from the porch, my tail started going back and forth, sweeping the tile. It sure would be fun to explore the new acres this summer, I thought. And when I'm out and about, maybe Rosy and I won't get in so much trouble, since we'll be on Evan's own land more often.

I've noticed on the farm, most everything kept growing until it died. Not necessarily people and animals, but they sure grow in wisdom and knowledge all the time. I suppose if they don't, then they get old like apples not picked on a tree and fall off. But nothing's forever, I guess. So my boss's farm grew. And expanded some more, almost each year. He seemed to keep ahead of the curve by producing more. I watched him work hard, putting in long hours, without much complaint. I think he liked farming more, and enjoyed the new relationships he had with farm owners.

Sometimes I heard him talking about buying a piece of property and taking out another loan. I could hear the worry in his voice about the increased risk he was taking on for the farm. I tried to take calculated ones, though, and I figured Evan did the same. Things seemed to keep working out, and the years went on.

We drove by the neighbors many times as we worked on the farm fields he owned or rented. I heard him saying they were doing some of the same. Of course this meant there were fewer neighbors, as some moved away to town for a job. Sometimes they were just getting old and decided to retire. Some stayed the same size, though, and got a job in town to supplement their income. I noticed some of the neighbors' wives drive by in the mornings and drive by again late in the afternoon.

My boss's friends from the city would come out, and I heard both parts of the couple had jobs there, too. It seemed everyone was working more and more all the time. Lucky for me, I could be with Evan while he worked. I'd hate being locked up in the house or backyard in the city while my boss went to work all day.

From time to time, a big truck would drive in with a larger tractor or harvest machine on board. The person would unload it and then load up a similar one that Evan owned. I loved to smell the new wheels after it was unloaded. While that was taking place, though, I would stop by a few wheels on the truck for the scent. Usually I paused to sort out the smell and then leave a little of my own. The truck had come into my territory, and I needed to make sure it knew where it was, even though I knew it soon would be rolling down the road again.

"Please sign here, sir. You've sure bought a nice one,"

"I know, isn't it something! I sure hope we can make the payments all right."

"Let us know if we can do anything for you, and I hope it works out," the driver said as he slid back into the seat of the semi-truck.

"Sure will, and thanks for the service. You guys do a great job keeping our equipment running when it's needed."

The driver left with a smile. My boss climbed up steps of the machine, opened the door, and looked it all over without closing it. I could smell the strong scent of "new" drifting in the air. I went up into a tractor at my boss's coaxing. It was a bit scary up there, but when he shut the door and got it moving, I was pretty surprised at the view from the buddy seat that was positioned by my boss.

Later, when I got out and headed down the steps, my toe got caught in one of the holes in the steel. With a big yelp, I hung by my foot for a second before Evan could rescue me.

There's not many times on the farm that he had to save me, and that seemed all backwards. I never climbed into a tractor again!

Watching this all play out over my years, it reminded me of a race that went faster and faster. Yet there didn't seem to be an end that I knew of, and the track just kept getting longer. Well, maybe that's okay, since we don't want things to end, but this one seemed different than most.

My boss kept successfully growing more from each acre he farmed, and he was farming more all the time too. The neighbors seemed to be doing the same. When we drove to town by the cooperative that stored some of the bushels at harvest for their farmers, we would see larger and larger piles of grain stored up under huge white tarps. I sure would like to play king of the hill on one of those piles, but I bet they would like my claw holes going all the way up! It seemed like farmers were doing some of the same scratching and clawing to get to the top of the pile themselves.

I wonder where it will end, I thought.

The Windstorm

The fall had turned out fabulous, almost too good to be true. I noticed the green crops turn a golden brown, as the sun matured them during the day, and the night offered them some rain to help the kernels fill out best. By this year, the farm had many fields. I had been to them all at one time or another, in the back of my boss's pickup truck. That was the best place imaginable for my sidekick and me.

There, we traveled through the countryside, with our noses busy, and our eyes on the lookout for other dogs, people, and maybe a varmint or deer that we might see. It seemed most times, Rosy was looking off the wrong side, but that's okay—I had keen eyesight and picked up what she missed. Most times we flew by without a chance to take on a chase, since my boss was usually on a chase of his own. It seemed he always had too many things to do. There were parts to get in town, and tractors to fuel up in the field in the fall. It was only glorious for us, and I think so too for my boss, sometimes. He was happy to work with his new crew to bring in the good production.

The crop was good that year, and the corn stood tall. The ears were massive and hung down along the plant, but plenty high enough that I could run under them. I could walk down the rows with my nose to the ground and not have to jump over even one plant that had broken over. The air was crisp.

Corn stalks and leaves that have matured put out a different smell that anyone would like.

Day after day, my boss would drive to the field and harvest. Sometimes I went and sat in the back of the pickup, hoping one of the crew would stop by. Then I'd get a pat on the head, and, if I was lucky, a treat from his lunch bucket. Sometimes a lady tractor operator would spend extra time with me.

The crew, when they gathered for a coffee break that my boss's wife delivered, had smiles on their faces and seemed to move quicker towards the lunch wagon. They gathered round the back of the SUV and politely took up a cookie and had a glass of tea or cup of coffee. This was the best time for me, since the pickings could get good. Sometimes I was the center of attention in the circle of folks, so I lay on my back and patiently waited for the belly rub that would surely happen. I'd turn my head with a short twist and look each one in the eye with a sparkle, thinking, *Are you going to be it?* Soon there was one, and maybe another would follow. The next afternoon, though, was a bit different.

"Did you all hear the weather forecast on the radio?" Evan said to the circle of crew.

"There's wind supposed to be coming up soon," looking at the app on his phone.

"Yeah, you can see it up north," one harvest operator said.

"It looks pretty gray. I bet the dust will be blowing here in a few minutes."

"The stalks are awful brittle, and the heavy ears seem to come off easy, don't they?" Evan said.

"That's for sure, when the machine hits them, they just fly," the operator replied.

"We better cut this break short, there's a long ways to go."

Sensing the tension, I quit asking for any treats or rubs and sat erect at his side.

They all climbed back in their seats in harvesters, tractor wagons, and trucks. I jumped back on the tailgate of the pickup, where Evan told me to go. There it was safe from the whir of the machines and the groan of the trucks as they left, laden with tons of corn. Dust drifted by my spot as they left the field and re-entered in a continuous cycle. All the equipment seemed to be moving faster than before.

I sensed something bad was about to happen.

* * * * *

Evan talked a lot about the changing weather. I heard it at night in the kitchen and during his morning coffee on the front porch with Ella.

"Honey, the storms are getting more severe in the summer, with the rain coming down harder. In the winter the weather seems warmer, and then a cold snap breaks all records," he said.

"You never know what's going to happen anymore, do you?" she quizzed.

"It doesn't seem so. Just hope for the best and prepare for the worst, I guess. Our equipment is in good shape and can get things done fast," he said.

"But Mother Nature is the boss," she replied with a tiny bit of a smile.

"You sure got that right, and we'll have to roll with her punches."

Getting punched doesn't sound good to me, but I'd sure like to see that old yellow tom cat get sucked up by a tornado, I thought while I plopped down on my side.

It was after lunch when the wind started blowing from the northwest. At first it was just a breeze, but soon it was a windstorm. The stalks started rattling like a shaker can of beads, while the dust began stinging my face. Leaves from the plants began floating by me. Since they were so dry, they came off easily. I could see the harvesters turn around and make another pass as the tractor wagons would follow to catch the golden flow.

They never stopped moving, and the harvester even unloaded on the go. Before long, though, I couldn't see them long after they turned, since the dirt was flying along with leaves and anything else that came loose from the ground. The wind was howling like a big pack of dogs. I hunkered down in the bed behind the tailgate that had been closed after lunch. It was a bit better there, but I hardly could breathe, so I tucked my nose in my fur some.

I knew a truck went by since I could hear its growl, but I barely noticed in sight since there was little to see but gray dirt and yellow matter in the air. Soon Evan rushed over. He had been in the truck, and said, "Get in here, Ace!" as he opened the cab door. It nearly came out of his hand, and he braced with his legs.

I jumped right over the tailgate to the ground and sprang to the door, leaping to his seat and over to the passenger side. He climbed in and slammed the door with both hands on it. I heard the two-way radio cackle in a more than normal scratchy tone.

"You better go look at that other field. That variety can break over easier," the guy said.

Evan grabbed the mic, and answered, "Okay, we might have to move over there and do what we can."

I had watched the procession of moving all the equipment and knew that took some time. My boss sped out of the field and down the road with both hands on the wheel. He was going west, and the wind blew him to the south side of the road, so he cranked it over sharply since he couldn't really see ahead of him much. At least I sure couldn't.

It wasn't too long, and he pulled into a driveway to scout over the field in question. Suddenly, he slumped in the seat and put his head down. He slowly reached for the handset, and put it to his face, while I waited upright, expectantly.

"Guys, it's too late. The field is all flat," he replied in a slow and methodical voice. "I'm sorry, but you may as well just stay there."

"Can we salvage any of it?" the voice responded

"Not much, and it's going to take three times as long to harvest what there is. It doesn't even look like there are rows anymore. The ground is going to be yellow with a myriad of ears."

I could pick them up and bring them to my boss, I thought.

The wind hit sixty miles per hour; I heard them say that day. It blew about the same the next, and then a little less the third day. That evening, it calmed down. My boss worked through it all each day. I stayed near the barn the rest of the time, since I didn't want to be in the way, and it was so nasty outside. My eyes burned, and I worked at night to claw the dirt out of my ears.

My boss said five fields were wrecked, with most stalks broken over. Myriad ears came off their shanks, and lay scattered all over the ground. There was nearly no way to pick them up.

"We could have been done in a week," he told Ella that night. "Now it will take three, since we can only harvest it one way, and we'll have to go terribly slow."

"Much worse, you'll harvest so much less," she replied.

I curled up in the corner of the kitchen that night, with my nose on my paw, and thought about the loss, and what it meant to holding the farm together. I sensed nature had taken another shot at my master, and I knew from my battles, each one takes a toll.

The Herd of Three Hundred

Evan had me around for another task, which was to be the head cow dog. When called upon, I played the role. Dashing at them with my volume full up was what it took to make the thick skinned and thickheaded beasts move. Being tough, and learning the circling maneuvers, were all part of it. One had to stay safe since I was outsized by a ton sometimes.

After the fateful corn harvest, large truckloads of cattle from out west were brought in to graze on the windblown fields. They were great at picking up the dropped ears. They would tip their heads back and roll the cob around in their mouths till the grain was all off. Their eyes kind of got soft and dreamy. I guess it was from eating tasty scraps all day long. That's another reason for not really liking them, not to say jealously is a virtue.

Though I was a shepherd, I was the small kind, and I wasn't really built for getting on the head or tail end of a cow. They had big hooves and hard heads, which they used to work you over with if they got you down. I knew the green material that sometimes came plopping out the back at random times, which really didn't excite me much either. One day, while chasing some out of the way of the pickup for my boss, I headed out after a few of the young heifers. Soon, I was dodging piles of green cow dung dropping incessantly while they were being chased. It was like land mines placed right in front of me!

The day came when my owner decided to put me in the back of the pickup and drive out to the well in the middle of the field to fill the water tank. All three hundred young cows were waiting around for a drink when we got there. It's probably a little like what the pioneers must have seen when the great herds of buffalo roamed the prairies. From the back of a pickup, or from the back of a schooner wagon like my forefathers, I bet the view was the same.

When we got to the big tank, my owner got out of our truck. I saw the heifers, and my owner called, "Come, boss," in his typical foghorn-sound voice, meant to carry a long way. Suddenly, with a chuckle, he ordered me to get out of the pickup by jumping off the tail gate.

I quivered a little, and looked over at him to make sure he wanted me to leap into that sea of cows. A little nausea developed. Though he knew my capabilities, he didn't seem to understand the risks to my hide, being dropped in the middle of three hundred black, brown, and white cows. It was a warm day, and the bovines seemed to be full of feed and rested up; now just milling around the salt and mineral licks my owner had placed for them earlier that week.

I thought, *No, you don't understand, boss,* but I only gave him a glancing look, not wanting to show him the concern I had. Of course, I was also worried about the open gate at the edge of the field. It would be my job to protect it, yet here I was surrounded by the critters. Sometimes Evan didn't think things through as well as I did.

When my owner called, I answered, and so I jumped. I found the perspective to be quite different from the ground level, surrounded now by six hundred beady eyes staring at me. My owner was done filling the tank. He stepped in his pickup and started driving off down the trail to the open gate. All of a sudden, a bawl went out from one of the cows closest to me.

She first put her head down at me, then a "two front foot brace position with tongue out" stance. The bawl seemed to ring out like an alarm siren to the entire herd. I decided that this would be a great time to go watch the gate and took off running as hard as I could, close behind the pickup. In hot pursuit were the cows. *Why do I gotta be the point of the joke?*

Suddenly my boss looked worried.

"Ace, get going, we have to get the gate shut before this whole herd gets on the road!" *There're cars coming and we can't afford to lose cows, much less get someone hurt,* Evan thought. *I shouldn't have been so foolish.*

"Run, Ace!"

These legs are going as fast as they can, I thought and offered him a reassuring bark in return.

I saw the two cars down the road in the distance. It looked to me like they were headed for a collision course with the dust makers. The only hope was that we make it to the gate in time.

I kept running trying to catch the pickup, and they kept coming. As I looked back, the dust cloud was getting bigger behind them. They had to travel the same distance to the gate, but they had a much longer stride. Ten times as much, I'm pretty sure. Worse yet, it was three hundred cows!

By the sound of the engine in the pickup, Evan had put his foot on the gas. I could see him look in the rear view mirror at the situation and once even put his head out the window. "Come on, Ace, you can beat 'em to the gate!"

I got another boost when boss urged me on, and I went into overdrive. But the cows just kept gaining a little more. My mind was racing as I thought, *This is all backwards!* as my back feet kept running into my front feet. I could see by the worried look on the face in the other mirror at the side of the pickup that I had to keep going. There was no time for him to stop and pick me up, or the herd would hit the gate before we did. I always thought cows were kinda dumb, but just leave a gate open for a bit, and you might think otherwise. It's like they have a sixth sense.

It seemed the sprint went on for about an hour in my hyper-focused little brain. Then suddenly there were only a few steps left, and we'd be at the gate. My boss hit the brakes just outside it. I leaped to the tailgate like a magnet to steel and took my stance. With all I could muster, given the wind left in me, I let out a huge bark and said, "Whoa, you bunch of overfed beef steaks!" I was suddenly eye to eye with all those cows, but only had to stop the first set of the pack.

"You're lucky we didn't pulverize you!" the lead heifer said.

"Not a chance, I was just trotting," I replied.

"Well, next time don't go bothering us when we're taking an afternoon nap," she bawled.

"You cows are no scarier than a flock of chickens!"

Evan jumped from the truck seat, grabbed the gate, and swung it fast shut. The cloud of dust drifted over us all, as the two cars whizzed by.

He looked at me kindly and said, "Good job, Ace," as he walked to the door.

Sure, boss, no problem. Coulda handled more, I thought as we headed out down the road with my front feet on the toolbox for a better view.

Losing Neighbors and Community

The landscape from the farm had changed a lot over the time I grew up. Dairies were some of the first ones to go out of business from the poor economic scene. Many of those places, marked by tall and round blue steel structures that held silage for cows, sat empty.

Farmsteads, like the one I lived on, had no one living there, and no farm operations going on anymore. People still lived on many of the places, and I spoke to their dogs at night. But few machines were heard at night during harvest or planting. The ones that were left were bigger though. Driving by an abandoned farmhouse in the evening with my boss left a pit in my stomach. I sure wished there were kids out in the front yards I could bark and wag my tail at when going by. Instead, tall weeds filled the driveways.

Evan told Ella, sitting in the passenger seat, on an evening drive, "We've driven by ten farmsteads in five miles, and I've realized there are only two families still farming!"

"Oh my, I think you are right", Ella replied. "Well, at least some of the families are still residing on them. They just must work in town for a living."

"But five of them are empty now and starting to fall down. No one is going to live in them again," Evan replied.

"Let's just have a nice drive and enjoy the scenery, Evan."

"Yeah."

My ears blew back easy in the wind while the breeze stirred my fur. It was almost as good as a petting. I thought about how it would have been back then. *Ten dogs in five miles, wouldn't that have been great!*

From my knowledge of the past owners of this place, I understood how hard it was to leave the farm. It seems the business got into a person's blood and became part of who they were. Evan was much more than that to me though.

"Do you remember this family, Ella," he asked as he drove by an empty farm, with only a driveway.

"Yes, but tell me more."

"I remember meeting the farmer. He had a family of kids and grandkids, and raised corn, cows, and a few hogs. Cattle were his pride, and he loved to see them line up at the bunk when he fed them corn to fatten them up for sale."

"I never met him."

"He had to quit farming one spring. I was young then, and looking for land to rent. I'd heard of his troubles and decided to find out if he might rent to me. I knew it was a good farm with deep, rich, black soil. So I stopped by one day and knocked on the door to meet the man and ask him," then Evan paused.

"How did it go, I don't remember?"

"He answered the door. He was a stout man, with a deep voice coming out under his moustache. He leaned on the old screen door, and said 'Hello'.

I told him I was a young farmer, and I'd heard his place might be for rent. Then I asked if we could work something out. He looked down, then right back up to me and said 'Maybe so'. Then our eyes met."

"Ella, I was standing there wondering if this old farmer was just being gobbled up. I was asking myself if I was part of the problem. Or am I just part of a grand plan to change farming? I didn't make him go broke, and I wished it was different, but I needed to make money and thought I could on this farm."

"I understand what you were thinking and going through, Evan."

"Remember we farmed it just a few years, and then the bank sold his land. It was probably the worst day of the man's life. I tried to console him, but it couldn't be done. I stopped by their house and talked to his wife at the kitchen table. She said he was too upset to even come out."

"As we drive by the place now, the buildings, including the house, are all gone. Only the driveway and the memories remain where it all stood. The bunks are gone, and so are the cattle. But the big field looks well cared for, with a new irrigation system in the middle. I bet lots of loads of corn will come from the place next fall."

"The old man didn't live long in town. His wife did, though, after he died."

"Is their house still there? We could drive by it when we go into town," Ella asked.

"No, even there they were asked to sell the house and property to make way for something else."

A while later, while still riding in the back of the pickup down the main street, I heard more through the open window.

"There's another business with a store closeout sale, Ella"

"I loved that little shoe store, Evan."

"They used to fix my work boots," he replied.

"Just as long as we don't lose the grocery store or the pharmacy."

"I'm worried about losing the parts store," Evan said.

Later that night we all settled in the house, and I thought, *I know a little math. Two out of ten—those aren't good odds for us. If my boss ever had to leave sight of the farm forever, it would be about the end of him too. As long as I could have sight of him, I'd be okay wherever we go, I guess. But, what if something happens to the farm, and then to him?* My head rested on both paws as I sat in the kitchen thinking about this. *In case it happens to me someday, I better be prepared. At least he'll still have me, and I'll try to make him happy.*

I glanced over to make sure he was still in his chair.

Badgering Badgers

Summertime on the farm was a glorious time. The weather sometimes offered cool mornings to go out, always on patrol for varmints. Then Evan might take a walk down the gravel road, which gave me an opportunity to flush something up out of the ditches or adjoining fields. By this date, Rosy was sleeping more and moving harder. She walked with both shoulders splayed out, and it looked like they hurt her, the way her tail went down some when she moved. Yet she would still be at my side when we needed to deal with a critter. I think her wisdom was becoming her real strength, and maybe even outsized her physical strength.

One of the more vicious and problematic beasts around the farm is a badger. They like to dig and dig everywhere, it seems. Many times there are holes in the field where they have tried to excavate a ground squirrel. Then the farm equipment has to bounce over them or, worse, break a wheel when it falls in. One day, I saw my Evan walking from a field to the farm shop.

"The darn hole broke off my planter wheel," he grumbled.

That was all it took for me to stay on high alert for these critters to rout them out

One day we ran into them along the road when Rosy and I were in the back of the pickup. My boss saw them and slowed down. There, just below his window, was a mother badger and six babies behind her. *That's going to make for a lot of holes someday,* I thought.

It was quite a sight, though. They all had bandit faces, similar to a raccoon. In fact, they kind of looked like a flattened raccoon without a tail! The mother and even the babies froze when they saw us.

She hissed at me, "Get out of here, you mangy dog," and then also hissed something at Evan.

"How dare you spit at him!" I said.

"How dare you get in my way!" she replied.

This was enough for war, just on its own, and I waited for my chance.

It was another hot summer day, and the corn was tall in the field on the other side of the fence. When Rosy flushed one out of the ditch near a hole in the bank, I went into action quickly since I didn't think she could handle one of these anymore. The critter, knowing it was in trouble, headed for the field to escape my wrath. We both pushed our way through the barbed wire fence, ignoring the scrapes, and then headed into the field in hot pursuit.

"Stop, Ace! I don't need any more vet bills!" he said.

"Sorry, boss, I've got to protect you from this varmint, and Rosy has already tagged it!" I barked, though I don't think he understood.

When I reached the beast, it looked to be a big one.

"Get lost, you crummy excuses for dogs," the badger hissed.

"Your hiss is a lot nastier than your bite, you lowdown hole-dwelling vermin!" I answered, though I remembered the story of Rosy, raising her pups in a hole too.

"Stop, dogs!" Evan yelled, but I pretended I couldn't quite hear him over the noise of Rosy barking and the badger hissing going on.

We will in just a minute, as soon as we're done, I thought. Sometimes you gotta take the bull by the horns.

We kept encroaching on the badger's space, keeping our distance and working to wear her out, since this was a good approach when dealing with something so strong. They say a badger will take on a human, and I sure didn't want that to happen here.

In a while we had worn the poor badger down to a frazzle. It was so wet with sweat, it was dripping. Rosy and I were still circling her and had knocked down a good few of corn plants in the effort. This didn't help much, since it let the sun in to beat down on us, and our tongues were both hanging out pretty far. The problem was, when I barked, my tongue had to go back in, or I'd end up biting it too!

The badger kept backing up as we were circling. I figured she knew where her earthly escape was. I knew it was time I to strike, or we'd have to dig her out.

"Just wait 'til I get to my hole, and I'll give you a face full of dirt on the way down!" she hissed.

"Not a chance!" I replied.

"Be careful!" Rosy barked.

That got the critter's attention, so I pounced on her when she was facing Rosy. She didn't know what hit her, I bet. Suddenly, though, between my claws and teeth was a tornado.

I'm not sure I've ever gone round and round with something like that before. Lucky for the badger, we rolled right to her doorstep, and down the hole she went.

"Well, I think we taught her a lesson, didn't we Rosy?" as I barked down the hole.

"From the looks of you, there sure was a lesson going on," Rosy replied.

I didn't know what she meant for sure. *Maybe I better not take on something so big and tough,* I thought. *One of these days I'm going to get really hurt.*

Taking the Bull by the Horns

In human time, I was now considered a mature adult. My boss had done plenty of watching me and Rosy take on varmints and critters by now. *I wonder if Evan learns from me*, I pondered. He sure encouraged us when the going got tough, and we needed a little support. He even broke up the fight if became too rough. I guess that's what his job was. We were protecting each other.

Now, I don't know, but I do remember him telling Ella, "That dog sure has courage!" after I had taken on the badger. I wonder if some of that courage rubbed off on when I jumped up on him at our morning greetings.

That evening after the harvest was in, supper was done and we were all sitting by the corn stove, he was texting with a farmer friend from a long ways away. I heard him mention the word "Illinois."

"Who are you texting, dear, and what are you talking about?" Ella asked.

"I'm talking to my friend Ken, who is getting pretty tired of the farm situation, and of losing neighbors, too. He's afraid he might be next, anyway. You never know what can happen," he replied.

"What are you going to do?" she asked.

"We're both going to get more involved in an organization that best represents our interests and the interests of farmers across America. It's pretty new and really seems to have a heart."

"But you've already spent a lot of time in Washington, and I miss you when you're gone," she replied. "Sometimes things get left undone here too."

"I'm sorry, and I hope you'll understand."

"I'll try."

"It's a big lift to try and change anything with agriculture policy. There are so many conflicting interests, and the food supply of our nation and that of some of the world is involved," he said.

"That sounds like a big animal to tackle."

I thought to myself, *Well, you've seen me take on some pretty nasty varmints, so you know it can be done.*

Evan looked down at me, stroked me on the head, and rubbed my ears a little as I lay beside him. I felt he was headed into some pretty difficult stuff, but I knew he had what it took, though I don't understand the "politics" critter much, and have never seen one.

The next week, I watched him carry out a suitcase from the house and kiss Ella goodbye.

"Have a good trip to Kansas City," she said.

"I'll be home Friday, after the meeting is over."

"Good luck. I'll be fine here."

No worries, boss, I'll take care of things while you're gone, I thought as I looked up at him obediently when he jumped in his truck.

I heard the sound of his pickup engine a few miles away late that Friday night, as I was sitting on the concrete porch steps. It was a good outlook post and allowed me to spring quickly to the sidewalk in case of a varmint alert. Rosy was lying behind me with her head in her paws, resting. *It's him!* So I sat up and readied for the lights to turn in the driveway, hoping it wasn't a rare instance where I was mistaken. But this time I was right.

With my little stump of a tail wagging, I jumped down to meet him at the garage driveway. He stepped out quickly from his truck, opened the back door, and pulled out his suitcase with a swing. "Hi, Ace! Good to see you, boy. Hey, Rosy, it's nice to be back after a busy week and long drive."

No worries, boss, everything is fine here, I indicated with a happy face and wiggling rump.

"I got some things accomplished, and I am sure glad you two held down the fort while I was gone."

I danced around a little, while Rosy sat at attention with her tail sweeping the driveway. She sure didn't move as fast as she used to.

"I better get in and see if Ella is awake."

She was, and I could see them kiss through the window of the back door that closed behind him.

The next morning, they let me in, and I overhead the talk at breakfast.

"Ken and I met with a group of people who represent a whole bunch of different farm organizations. They all seem to have the same thing in common - that is, a worry about a decent farm economy, and the ability to manage the supply and price of what they produce."

"So what are you going to do?" she asked.

"We're going to organize," he said.

A Rosy Life

Rosy was a well-bred black Labrador of the retriever family. She really didn't have any "farm dog" in her like I did. Yet she had developed those skills to a good degree. Her retrieving was best in the water, and she swam as fluid as the liquid around her. If my boss threw a stick in the water, she would leap from wherever she was, and make a line to the object with mostly her head and nose in view. Sometimes she would quickly change course, if the current or the wind moved the object out of her line. You could hear the air rush out of her nose as the water churned around her from her feet paddling. These were all her best days. The full body shake back on shore seemed to shed nearly all the water off her thick coat. But those days were over, it seemed.

Rosy loved to dig for gophers on the front lawn. My memory of this was in the waning days of these critters on the farm, since Rosy and her earlier sidekick had nearly eradicated them. The front lawn was kind of minefield because of it. It took a lot of digging to extract one of them, and there were numerous entrances to the labyrinth of tunnels the gophers had built. A gopher needs plenty of escape routes when it crosses a lawn with a couple of overzealous dogs after him. I still notice the lawnmower and operator lurch when they hit one of these old battle zones that left a hole in the yard. Typically, I wouldn't even have to look from the porch. I could just hear the muttering of Evan when he hit one of them. It wasn't my fault, though, since I hadn't been much a part of it.

The digging for these critters, along with the rabbit hunting, and battling other varmints, had taken its toll on Rosy. She walked much slower now, and couldn't run. Sleeping seemed more of a priority than hunting. When I took off after a varmint, she would lunge forward, and then stop.

"That's okay, Rosy, I'll take care of it for you," I'd say, seeing her hurt quite a bit. So I did my job extra hard to cover for her. Evan gave her some medicine to treat her every day. It seemed it helped some, but still Rosy was not her typical old self. Her jet black muzzle had white hair mixed in now.

I really hadn't experienced old age ever before, being young myself and not having been able to see my parents grow old. Most varmints around here seemed young and spry when we chased them. Evans kids weren't that old, either.

When I walked by her spot and saw her sleeping, I took an extra look at her and set my paws down easy so as not to disturb her. Sometimes she would hear me anyway, and our eyes met when she woke. It was a more stoic look, it seemed.

"You know I won't be around here forever, don't you, Ace?"

"Not really."

"Every living thing has an end, Ace. Your mother probably never got to that with you before you left."

"Nope. That just makes me think of tail ends."

"This is more serious. I'm at the beginning of the end."

"Why don't you stop it; chase it off?"

"Because I can't. All I can hope for is to slow it down."

"Like a race to the end? Slowing that down doesn't make sense."

"Ace, it's not a race, and it's not a tail. I'm talking about the end of my life, and someday even the end of yours."

"Oh."

That thought had never entered my mind. *Maybe the circle of life they talk about is like the circles I make chasing my own tail. All this thinking is making me dizzy too.*

From then on, I watched Rosy with some concern, interest, and sadness. I'm not sure this was right but this is what I felt, since Rosy told me it was a natural thing. Yet, it looked like I was getting close to losing a friend. *I guess "the end" can split friends up. That seems too bad. But I could still have the memories of us. Rosy didn't say they had an end.*

"Where are you heading to this morning?" she would ask as I trotted down the front sidewalk.

"I'm going for a run up the road with the boss, but it looks like you don't feel very good." I said. "Maybe you better stay put today, and we'll go on afternoon patrol around the place later together," I continued.

I knew it hurt her now, to go down the road, and wanted to discourage her.

"Thanks. I think I'll rest a little. Don't let any badgers get you."

"Not a chance in a hundred years," I said. *I hope she gets another year. I don't know what I'll do without her.*

Everything will be okay, I thought. Such an eternal, confident, optimist I was! Death wasn't something I had dealt with much. I had done battle with about everything and mostly won, but this was much different. It seemed pretty simple, *you're here and then you're not.* Yet, it felt ominous, like losing something very precious.

That summer morning started out like most other hot summer days, with me sitting on the front porch keeping guard. Rosy came over and walked up the steps late, moving very slowly by me to her position. I saw her gait, and a wave of worry hit me. When she walked by me, I asked "How are you today, girl?" by wagging my tail.

I panted a bit to try and perk her up. There was no reply from her, which was a little unusual. *She's not doing well at all and I don't know what's going to happen. How will I get along on the farm without her?*

As the morning waned, Rosy headed down the steps and into the bushes on the north side of the house. This was a favorite place for her, where she could lie in the cool dirt swale she had dug for when it was hot outside. It seemed a bit early for this, but these were the lazy days of summer.

Evan had seemed worried about her for the last several days. "How are you doing, Rosy?" Evan asked as he went by. He paused a bit and attentively looked at her. Then he patted her a little bit more and talked softy to her.

Rosy had a look on her face, resting on her front paws, which I hadn't seen before.

The morning passed with no varmint appearing, yet I felt as tense as I had ever felt. I did feel relieved that nothing had shown up, since I really wanted to be by her today. I rested on the sidewalk outside the bushes by her spot and lay there panting some. It was even hotter, and I still had my heavy coat on, but also I usually panted when I was anxious, like when a thunderstorm popped up and lightning flashed, though I know I shouldn't be so scared of them.

Rosy rustled a little and groaned. It sounded just like thunder to me at that moment.

"Are you okay?"

"As alright as I'll ever be."

I cringed, like something was attacking me.

For once, my world at this moment was just centered on Rosy. It wasn't about the next varmint, or my boss, or Ella, or even Clara.

"You know I've tried to teach you all I could, don't you?" she said.

"Yeah, I know. And even though some of those lessons were pretty distasteful,"—*especially the toad experience*—"I'm sure glad I learned them from you," I said.

"Yes, I was a little hard on you sometimes."

"It's okay,"

I swept my tail on the sidewalk as I sat there. I decided to go get a drink of water at the water tank, and check in at the barn to make sure the cats were minding their own business, and not my dog dish. *I better get back soon,* and figured I better lie down there and spend a little while. But I did leave for a bit and walked slow. Maybe it was because I didn't want to see it happen, or maybe it was because I just wanted to think about all the good times we had together. It probably was some of both. Being such close companions, I knew she knew why I left too.

Evan and Ella had come outside after lunch. They were unusually quiet and began looking for Rosy. She didn't respond to their calls. I didn't think they'd seen her go in the bushes earlier that morning. I decided to be brave and take it on myself to go check it out. They called for Clara who was inside.

"Clara, where is Rosy? Have you seen her this morning?"

"No, dad, I haven't, but she's been laying in the bushes a lot lately."

I led the way for them to her.

When I went closer to the bushes where Rosy had been, I sensed something. My feet immediately slowed down to a crawl, almost like they knew she was dead. I put my nose in the bushes and could see her, but she smelled so different. I breathed very little but studied each breath, for its scent and complexity. It was the smell of death that I knew from my instinct. I hadn't smelled that before in a dog, and especially in one I loved. I stopped in my tracks to study it, and her. Rosy didn't move. Storms raced in my head. I felt like I was drowning in a pool of water. I tried to get around it, but it wouldn't leave my senses. I knew it would always be there in my mind. But my old sidekick Rosy had brought it to me. *She just gave me her last lesson,* I thought, as I moved away and decided to go for a walk down the road, this time alone. There was the horizon line along the hill. It was still, and warm, and the sun was shining. *I'm in full charge now.* The weight of my body on my legs seemed heavier but my mind strengthened and told me I was ready to carry the load.

From my vantage point, a bird in the clear sky swooped low between the old house and the row of green spruce trees close by at that moment. It was gray, and I think Evan called that type a Mourning Dove.

When I came back, I saw Evan pick Rosy up very carefully and take her away. I heard his heavy breath in the grove of trees close by the shop and could smell fresh earth. I stayed on the porch.

Evan showed up again, walking slowly to the place where I sat. He knelt down and gave me a good scratch under my chin, along with a soft stroke on my head. I rolled over and he rubbed my belly. I returned with a lick to his hand.

"It will be okay, Ace. I just realized the marking on your chest looks like a heart when on your back."

Seems when things are upside down is where we find ourselves, I thought.

He then walked quietly into the house, and the door closed behind him.

At that moment, I wasn't so sure any more that things will work out. Maybe sometimes they just don't. Or maybe that was just how things work out sometimes.

The next morning the sun came up as I sat on the front porch, just as usual. It was bright and pretty, and it was a bit cooler in the air. Today, I was the head farm dog, and this felt strange. It was like some of Rosy's age and wisdom had suddenly been instilled in me. I scanned the horizon line for critters with extra intent, as I listened hard for the steps of my boss in the house headed for the door. I wanted to be at full attention when he came out to greet me, and I was.

"How are you doing this morning, Ace?" he asked.

I tipped my head up and gave his hand a reassuring lick after he stroked my head.

Something new is ahead of us, and I'll be ready for it, I thought.

Beans

I'm sure Evan knew I needed an assistant. To this date, he always had one as well. First, I think it was Jamie. But he was going to be gone now, most of the time. Then it was his younger sidekick, Clara, who rode horses with him and met him in the barn every night to feed us and do other less important things like petting the cats. But she got bigger as I stayed the same, and then she was soon to be gone, too. I heard them talk about college, and knew what happened with Jamie when they did before.

I wonder if they would ever send me off to school, I thought. I figured not, given how much I already knew and that I was now senior. There was certainly more than one way to learn though!

For a little while it was me and the cats in the barn at night. *I thought cats were supposed to eat mice for a living,* ran through my mind, as Clara put out cat food in a dish for them. After they left, and if I jumped high, I could get on the bale pile where they placed the bowl away from me. It was game on then, with felines scurrying everywhere as I cleared the decks so I could eat cat food in peace.

"Clear out, you lazy cats," I said. "Why don't you go make some mincemeat out of some mice over in the trees?"

"Yeah, sure," the gray striped cat said. "But wait till your boss sees you up here eating our food."

"I didn't think a dog like you wouldn't lower himself to eating from a cat dish," the calico mother cat said. "Nothing like taking food from my babies."

"That's hitting below the belt," I muttered, since I hadn't thought of it that way before. It was kind of hard to swallow the next mouthful.

A few months after Rosy was gone, Clara gave me a hug and a pat, and drove down the road in her car. I didn't see her all that weekend or the next week, even. Evan had a tired smile on his face, so I tried my best to rub him up. The next week, I made an extra effort to nuzzle him when I could, and ran fast when he called.

"You're a good dog, Ace," he said. "She'll be back."

I wagged my tail at that thought.

That fall day, when I rode to the big city with Evan, he stopped at the building that had all kinds of dog and cat smells coming from it.

I wonder if this is the dog pound. Wow, this has to be the lost and found department.

Evan smiled and said, "Stay put, Ace, I'll be right back."

He seemed to know the place, like he'd been here before.

He had an even better smile on his face when he came out, and I smelled a different dog on his hand when he petted me.

"Thanks for coming back, and I bet you'll enjoy her. She's been a good dog here," the lady at the door said.

About a week later, I was over by the barn when Evan drove in with his pickup. Beside him on the seat was a dog! I didn't know what to feel, but I sure did know what to do, having been on the other side of this in my early years when I was the new guy. So that's what I did, and it seemed to be the thing to do. The sniffing, posturing, and circling all worked out.

He called her Beans. I figured out that she was a she when we did the sniffing thing. She was a medium-sized dog with a long, curled-up kind of bushy tail. Black turned to grays and tans all over her. Her face was perfectly proportioned with these colors, and she had a bright eye. Chestnut brown, I would call them. All her legs were tan, with black short claws poking out. Beans was a sharp-looking dog, if I had been looking for a mate—but I was fixed. She never growled once at me during the interaction, and her tail stayed up, but not too far up. No hair stood up on her back either. Right away, she trotted over to the barn, and I could see her interest in the cats as her tail came up further, and she gave them some stiff turning glances. *That's my kind of dog,* I thought.

"Whattya do with all these cats around?" she asked.

"Keep them in line the best I can," I replied as I nabbed one by the scruff and dropped it outside the barn. It wasn't long before Beans was helping me guard the place and keep the cats out of our respective dog dishes.

Beans would jump up in the morning to greet "our" Evan with a wagging tail and a tongue hanging out many times. It was her happy face, as she looked up at him while he reached down to pet her. He walked over to the shop to do some work, I suppose.

"How about we go for a run?" she asked.

"Without our boss?" I responded.

"Sure, why not?"

"Because I've got a farm to watch out for."

"Well, there's a lot out there to see, and we're not going to see it from the porch," she replied. "Let's explore the creek we drove by a few miles east."

"Are you kidding? Do you know how mad Evan would get if he caught us?"

"Oh, quit worrying. We'll be back before he notices were gone," she replied, and then bounded off the porch.

Good grief! I better follow her and make sure she stays out of trouble! I thought; admittedly with a bit of excitement running through my veins.

I'm not really sure where she lived before or what she did, and even if she had a job.

I did wonder if her type of spirit ended her up in the dog pound, as I ran to catch up with her.

We made it to the creek and back before our boss noticed. When he came back to the house there we were sitting on the porch all muddy and tired.

"Where have you two been?"

Both our tails wagged profusely as we sat there

One night, only about a week after she arrived, we were both sitting on the front porch on duty. Beans had been telling me about her travels, some even as far as across the river. "So is that what landed you in the dog pound? I asked.

"The first time, it was," she said as she put her head into her paws.

"How'd you get out?"

"A kid from town came and rescued me."

"How long were you there?"

"A month," she said as she lay over on her side and didn't move.

Wow, I thought to myself. *A month is a long time.*

"Sure was a long stretch," she said.

"So how did you land in there the second time?"

"The kid was young, and had to move somewhere and couldn't take me along."

"That's a bummer," I said.

"You got that right. More time in the slammer."

"But you didn't do anything wrong!" *Though I wonder why somebody else didn't take you. Maybe they knew your reputation of being kind of a free spirit.*

"Nope, was just being myself," she said as she sat back up.

"So how long were you in there that time?"

"Two months."

"Dang"

"Yeah, the good thing was that a kind old man fed me every day and cleaned my kennel.

Once a week he would take me outside on a leash, and we would walk around on the grass for a while. He would rub me all over and comb out some of my last year's fur that was still hanging on. I think that's why I didn't get adopted, because I still had some scraggly hair."

"How'd Evan find you?"

"He stopped by one day, and paused to look at me. Our eyes met, and he asked the old man if he could take me outside for a bit". "How are you, girl? You sure seem good on a leash ", he said.

"I was so happy, and I tried my best to be very polite. When he kneeled down beside me, I tucked right in between his legs."

"That musta done it."

"I think so. The third time he stopped in, we went outside, and I left for good."

"I think I was there for the second, but had to wait in the pickup. I'm glad it's over for you now."

"Me too."

After that night, we both just lived some, keeping our noses pointed forward. Though when I studied her eyes when she was scenting something, I could almost see a roadmap of the places she'd been. There was a depth and a wildness in her that made me worry a bit, especially if I was following her. But the only thing I really worried about was my job and Evan, and the farm. Of course I always worried about thunder when I smelled a storm. *I guess I worry quite a little, but I won't ever worry about a dog pound since I know Evan would always come and get me.*

Beans had a few things she actually taught me soon enough. She didn't worry about anything, other than the dog pound. Not lightning, or thunder, or the turn around the bend. When Evan called her, she came, with a confident trot. She would lie alone by the barn, and not really need my company. Maybe her traveling days did that to her.

Beans would walk confidently by the horses in their stalls in the barn, with their heads sticking out. She never dropped her tail, which was in reach of their teeth, and I never heard a yelp like they took a crack at it. She had an air about her that seemed to work.

She greeted others nearly same way. Like the other guy who worked on the farm and drove in the yard nearly every morning - he let her jump up on him and do a little roughhousing, which I was never allowed to do.

I learned from all that. So I figured this was going to be a pretty good gig between Beans and me. That is, if I kept us out of trouble.

Winter soon came, after the harvest and all the excitement of a new sidekick. We had settled in together pretty well by then. Since she was older than I had been when coming onto the farm, and due to our size difference, we became more of equals. She had the outward-bound experience, and I had the farm gig down.

Sometimes, this season got a little dull for us. Evan would spend lots more time in his office "counting beans", as I heard him say to Ella one time. I think that meant sizing the finances of the farm up after a year of growing crops and bringing them in. I sat outside his office many times, on the sunny south side, and could hear the printer tape of a calculator clicking along. He would come out of his office mid-morning and carry some papers to the mailbox, or maybe to his house, then come back with some more in his hand. It seemed like it was all about paper. During those times, he seemed distracted and ignored me some. I forgave him for that, since I could see by the creases that had formed on his face that there was plenty to worry about on the farm, and the papers must have been a big part of it.

Many times, I could see through the frosty window that he was standing by a screen full of numbers that kept flashing and changing. On snowy days, he would come outside with a broom and sweep the satellite dish clear that was mounted on the wall of the building and pointed towards the sky. I wondered if it was a big ear, or something, like I had.

When I got really bored, I would move closer to the front door of the office, in case he came out, not wanting to miss a second of him being with me. Beans was still a little more aloof and was happy to lie in the snow somewhere, like she had a bit of Husky in her. Of course, with my heavy coat, I was ready for anything except the Arctic. I had heard of that place, and also of the white polar bears covering their noses in waiting. That sounded like too big a varmint.

Sometimes the door of the office would slam hard when Evan was leaving for lunch, and I'd hear him grumbling about "bear markets." That didn't sound good, and he didn't look good either. He also talked about the market hitting the limit, with a disgusted look on his face, and that also didn't sound good. Some days he came out and was perkier, with a bit of a spring in his step. I wonder if it all had something to do with that big ear on the building wall. *Maybe I ought to just chew through the cord going to it,* I thought. *Then he wouldn't be so busy and worried all the time.*

I talked to Beans about it one day.

"I thought farmers spent all their time growing crops and fixing fences outside," she said.

"Well, I guess you've got a few things to learn on the farm," I replied. "I heard Boss say that the farm is made or lost in the office once."

"That's why he spends so much time there, I guess," she said.

"Beans is beans, and I guess he's got to count them to make sure the farm will have enough," I said.

"Well, he's got me."

"That's not the same, silly! We're talking about money - the stuff that makes the world go 'round."

"I guess you're right. We gotta look out for the obstacles ahead of us," she said. "Like the river to the north."

Soon, I began to understand that Evan was doing a little bit of what I did: guarding the farm. That was probably why he was so intent when he came from the office. He was watching out for financial dangers that might hurt the farm. I suppose he, too, had to make some quick moves to avoid bad things, acting fast when he had to.

I stepped back for a bit. *What's the next danger going to be for me?*

At least I knew I would have Beans by my side.

Coonhound Fevers

Not much different than my boss dealing with unsavory characters or markets that rob him of hard-earned profits, a dog needs to watch himself or he'll get into trouble pretty easily. I had always worried a bit about getting really hurt by a critter. Then I wouldn't be able to take care of the farm and things might go bad. Of course, I wondered a little about my life too, and didn't want to go wherever Rosy went.

The day I took on a great big raccoon, across the road in the trees, turned out to be a pretty tough deal. Beans stood back with a look of wariness, so I had to take most of the load. I'm not sure what she had in her past that caused this hesitation but I figured there was something. *Or maybe she's just wiser than I am,* I thought.

The critter was a mean, nasty, pungent-smelling thing, probably with a home up in the cottonwood tree near where we ended up wrangling. It had decided to come down during the day, which was a big mistake when I was around. I jumped it first, planning on Beans coming in right behind me. Well, she did, but not until I was deep in the battle. There was a point where I felt I was being dragged down a gravel road, or so my face looked after the swipes the darn critter took at me. But I shook it off and kept on wrangling. It was rougher than rough. If you could imagine being in a clothes dryer, with leftover nails

215

from your boss's jeans pocket, that would be about it. There were jabs and bites here and there, wet everywhere, and two fur coats going 'round and 'round. By the time it was over, I think both me and the critter had taken enough.

Beans and I headed back across the road to lick our (mostly my) wounds and get a drink of water. I think I was a little worse for wear after I sized myself up a while after settling down. Sometimes, when the adrenaline rushes, I can't even feel the claws and bites, yet when Evan accidently steps on my paw, I yip! That's a curious thing about danger and adversity. I don't realize how much I can take until I face off with the threat at hand.

Well, the side of my nose had lost all its hair, and my lip was torn and swelling on the nose area. I was limping from a paw wound. One of my own claws was torn, I suppose from a big swipe I took at the beast, or perhaps from one of his strikes. I hurt all over.

"Oh Ace, we better get you to the veterinarian," Evan said as he looked me over handling me gingerly.

I think that would be a good idea boss, as much as I hated the place.

When we got there, those terrible disinfectant smells, mixed with medicines and the mournful kennel sounds, hit me in the face when my boss opened the front door. I did a quick think, then a one-eighty turn, but what is a dog to do when he is hurt? Licking wounds goes a long way, so when Evan yanked on my leash I sat down and started in earnest, hoping my boss would get the idea, or so I thought.

"So, what did you get into, boy?" the vet asked, as he looked at my face.

I pulled back when he felt my nose and cleaned it with a gauze pad and some of that disinfectant.

"Easy there, tiger, we've got to make sure you don't get infection," he said.

I'll be alright, I tried to tell him with my eyes. *"Just let me go home, and maybe Evan will give me a bowl of milk for the night, since my mouth is kind of worn out."*

"You'd better stay here overnight," he said with a look in his eye.

Evan picked me up the next day. I'd had a few stitches, a shot in my bum, and he had been given some pills to feed me. I sure hoped he'd put them in some raw hamburger (kind of what my nose looked like) instead of giving me the "pill pushed down the throat" treatment. I spent the night on the back porch and slept pretty well, dreaming of the magnificent battle the afternoon before.

In a few days, I felt better. And after a week, I was back to full speed.

Then one morning, I felt a little stiff and weak again. I got up from my bed in the bushes, but my front legs just didn't seem to work very well. Evan saw me and looked a bit worried, so he checked the legs out, but there wasn't anything to see on the outside.

Beans asked, "What's wrong with you?"

"Don't know, but I'll be all right." I was thinking of the vet office again.

"I'll bet you'll be taking a trip in the morning," she replied.

I gulped, and thought of the infection the veterinarian had mentioned. He had said something to Evan about the "deadly risks" of that.

By afternoon, things were getting worse, and I couldn't really move my back legs very well either. The next morning I woke, tried to get up, and nothing happened. It was like my brain wasn't connected to my legs or paws. By chance, I'd slept out in the trees, a ways from the barn and house. I decided to try and bark to get someone's attention, but nothing came out. This felt like real trouble. So I decided I was going to have to get to some help myself. With the type of effort that I store up for big battles and big deals, I dragged my limp body a few feet at a time towards the house. I heard Evan calling for me, but I couldn't do a darn thing about it but keep crawling. In time, I reached the house, and Evan saw me. With a horrified look on his face, he scooped me up and lay me in the pickup seat for another drive to the vet clinic. It seemed he was driving faster than normal.

"Ace, what's wrong with you? What happened?"

I'd tell you if I could, Boss, I thought.

Again, I faced the anxiety over the smell at the door, but all I could do was look at Evan. There, the experienced vet looked me over again. I must admit his hands felt kinder. *I'm glad he's trying to help me.*

He examined my legs and back, and tried to get me to move but I couldn't. Standing back he put his hand to his chin and thought.

"I'm afraid your dog has a disease of the nervous system called coonhound paralysis," the veterinarian said. "It's quite serious, and there isn't much we can do for it, but with luck he will start getting better in a few weeks."

"So, you think he got it from the fight with that raccoon the other day, Doc?"

"Most likely. It's believed to be carried in their saliva. Dogs that chase them have a susceptibility to it. When they come down with it, they become almost completely paralyzed."

"Well, that's sure fits this one."

How was I to know? And what was I to do? I can't let them run over the place. I sure didn't like the talk of just maybe getting better. Nothing - nothing - in my life had ever stopped me in my tracks; and this thing most literally had.

For the moment, I succumbed to my current fate. *So much for recovering from my earlier injuries, only to be hit by this delayed attack.*

I stayed in the vet hospital for a week. All I could do was raise my head and wag my tail. I could eat some and drink water, if they got it close enough to me. They lay me on an absorbent pad. Thankfully, these people understood which side was up. At least I could pick up my tail a little when it came to "doing my duty", with hopes someone would come in and clean up things quite often.

Mostly I thought, *How was I going to get revenge on this creature that put me in such bad shape? But what is the use of revenge, anyway? Didn't the varmint win fair and square? And even if it didn't, what was the use of getting back? I mean, unless the critter would attack Evan, or one of the farm animals, I guess there is little point in revenge. And that wouldn't even be revenge, but simply defense. That's all I'm about—protecting what I'm supposed to.*

So I threw out the idea of revenge and spent my time working on getting better.

Wouldn't the world be a better place if we dropped the word "revenge" altogether? I thought.

Evan took me home again, as I was looking a little less weak, and they put me in the warm shop building since it was winter. There I lay for days, sometimes able to drag myself a few feet in the hopes of getting up on them and outside, where I longed to go - but to no avail. So I decided to use all my courage and just tough it out, not knowing how long it would take, or if I would ever recover.

Lying there all that time, I thought, *I've got to be patient.* So I dreamed of rabbit hunts to help pass the slow time, and make the best of it. I learned that loneliness isn't all that bad, since I had myself and a mind to work with. Being such an independent dog all my life, I felt so helpless in that situation, yet grateful for the care Evan and his family gave me. A light turned on inside me one night in the dark. I realized that accepting help is about as valuable as offering help. There wasn't much else to do except listen to the radio they had on close by, or hope for someone to come and see me. Accepting their care more easily now, I licked any hand I could reach.

"How are you, Ace?" Clara said, stopping in one evening for feeding. She was now home from college, and on Christmas winter break.

Just fine, as I looked up at her with the saddest eyes I could muster, thinking I could get another belly rub.

One morning, a week or so later, Evan tried to stand me up. He held me gently, and with all the strength I could muster, I tried to hold myself on my rubbery legs. I did. Before long, I was taking a few steps, and in a week, I was walking a little. *Day by day I'm a little better. Looks like I'm going to make it.* In a month's time, I was trotting down the road.

So, as much as I hate to say it, that darn coon taught me a few things. I don't think that's how it had planned things to work out, but so it did. I now know what I can get through, and know what it is like to be in a hospital. Beans was kind to me while I lay there. She never ate my food, and sometimes licked my fur when I couldn't. It was a hard way to get a lesson but it sure was a learning experience. Just like my sidekick, Rosy, had taught me along the way.

In the end, I was able to trot down the road with Evan on his exercise run, as I had been used to doing. It was really good to be better.

A Prescription for Farmers Delivered in a Station Wagon

The next year went by fast, and I recovered to my old self through it. By fall I was as fit as ever, and resumed all my duties with full strength, though maybe I wasn't quite as strong or quick, given my age.

One day, as the boss was working on some farm equipment before harvest started, an old beat up car drove in. The car was about as dusty as the road behind it. I trotted over to be near the event. My rump wiggled some, and I hoped that the visitor would be nice. This seemed the case right away, as the old gentleman smiled at me when he got out of his car. I noticed things piled up high in his back seat, and wondered if there would be any room for a dog, if he had one. His license plate had a desert scene on it, so I figured he was from a long way off. Beans followed, and we shared sides of the car to check out the tires. My tail went up from all the scent on them.

"Hello, sir, my name is Clarence, and I drove here to talk to you since I hear you know a thing or two about the farm situation," he said.

My boss wasn't much for traveling salesman stopping by unannounced, and from the first look on his face, I figured that's what he thought he was.

"We better get our wheel checking over quick," I told Beans as I lifted my leg.

But when Evan heard the man talk about the farm, his head went up, and his eyes were more directed at the man. There was a serious look in my boss's face.

"You have? Well, you've come a long ways, from the looks of it."

"Yes, but this is important," the man said. "I understand how to fix some things, and want to share them with you. Your name is getting to be known around."

Evan looked down at the ground for a moment, and then picked his head up. "Tell me, then."

"I've spent my whole life in agriculture, and wanted to tell you about my plan to solve the problem of low prices for farmers," Clarence said.

"I understand that situation quite well," Evan replied. He seemed reflective, as he rearranged the dirt with his boot tip in front of him.

"Do you know that the business of farming is quite unique in the world, and that it really functions under a different system than many others?" Clarence said.

"Well, I know the buyers kind of have a monopoly on the market, it seems."

Hmm, I've watched the family play that game during the Christmas holiday season when everybody was home. It always caused a crazy scene on the floor between the players!

"You're partly right," Clarence said. "But you actually work in a monopsony, because the buyer has control of the market and the money. Better said, it is actually an oligopsony, because there is more than one buyer, but really only a few major ones that control a good part of the sales in the world, actually."

Those are some pretty big words. I sure like the idea having control of all the dog bones around here, licking my lips with that thought.

"Is that so? I guess you're right on that point. I could name the principals on one hand of fingers."

"Worse yet, you have no ability to control how much all the farmers produce yourself. You may not raise a thing on this farm, but the country may still raise more than they need, and prices will still be cheap."

"So I have to produce all I can even if the prices are low, since my only choice is to raise more and sell more."

"That's right."

"That's why we need our government to help us with some framework that lets us manage our supply, and also make sure we have enough when production is down due to a drought or something."

"You're absolutely correct," the old man said. "Further, though, you might not know how much of a balance it is between the supply and the demand. It's kind of like a teeter-totter at the park, at resting level. Imagine putting just a scoop of sand on one side?"

"That side goes down much further than you think it might, and the other goes up higher as well. Also, you forgot to mention how heavy of a hand the big grain companies have in the marketplace. They can tip the scale easily to their favor."

"That's what I meant when I talked about a monopsony or oligopsony, which is control of the market by the hands of a few instead of one. You have to remember that the business of food production and farming are unique," he reiterated. "We can't run out of food, or we're in trouble, and our government knows it."

"Those are sure some big words, Clarence."

"They are, and they have even larger effects."

I thought, *I sure don't want to run out of dog food, but if I did, at least I could go catch a rabbit or something. I guess the dogs in the city would have a harder time with that, though.*

"I've got to think on this Clarence. If you're right then, well, I guess we need to get our groups together, and go to Washington to explain this uniqueness to them. Maybe then they will work to pass a farm bill that does the right things, and protects farmers and consumers of food. It seems there can be a balance that is fair for everyone." My boss had quit scratching in the dirt with his boot. He stood up tall and looked out to the horizon.

"This would be just what the doctor ordered - a new prescription for agriculture," Clarence said.

There was a handshake and goodbyes, then a cloud of dust behind the old station wagon that headed east from our farm. I wondered if he would stop again, and I thought that he was a bit unique himself.

Market Crashes

That next winter I was fine but it seemed my boss wasn't. He would walk past me and say, "Hi, Ace," but not take the time to reach down and stroke my head like he used to. I wondered if his mind was in a far-off world like Beans seemed to be sometimes, while she was lying on the porch.

The market screen seemed to be a place where he spent a lot of his time when I followed him to his shop office. We trudged through the snow while I listened for other animal life. I didn't hear much at all, since the snow muffled sounds. There were no tree leaves to rustle, and the squirrels were sleeping in their winter nests near the tops of the cottonwood trees. It was the dead of winter. *Maybe everything is just sleeping,* I thought. Evan also seemed sleepier and spent more time in his black recliner in the living room. I didn't mind, though, and just slept some myself on the floor rug that centered the room.

The next day we went out to the office again like usual. My boss turned on the screen and, as normal, scanned the news section first. I lay just a few feet away, keeping my eye on him in case he decided to head out the door and jump in the pickup, since I never wanted to miss a ride.

Suddenly, he stepped back and stood at complete attention staring at the screen. I could see his head turn from side to side as he sped through the lines of text.

"Embargo on China, and a trade war started," he said quietly while continuing to read. His fingers moved to another button, and the screen switched to the one that always had the numbers scrolling by. Some days they were mostly green or maybe mixed green and red. This time, all I could see was red. Also, instead of single digits in red, these digits were all double.

Evan gasped.

I wondered about the farm again.

"It's collapsing," he said. "What are they doing to us?"

He walked away from the screen and sat in his office chair. It rocked back, and I lost sight of his face, but he was quiet, and he just sat there and didn't move.

I smelled his sweat in the room.

The Canyon's Long Divide

It's surprising how things can compound on themselves. Fleas in my doghouse are a prime example. Or watching Evan try and hold the farm together through rough times. One mistake can cause an even bigger mistake. Or a problem that can't be solved before it causes another.

The spring had been dry, but we got the crops planted all right. Market prices were terrible, though, and I could see the lines get deeper on my boss's face.

"Why don't you just get away and go fishing for a few days?" Ella said.

"Yeah, that's what my father used to do in the spring when it was too dry to plant," he replied. "Then it always seemed to rain."

In his eyes, I could see the look of hope, and a brightness developing, and I knew he was going fishing. Certainly, he would be missed but I would cover the best I could while he was gone.

The grain market was down that day, and there was no rain in the forecast. I'd hear him lament that his farm bill proposal was going nowhere. I thought, *How do you go nowhere?* I figured that nowhere was at least somewhere. With all this on his mind, he loaded his pickup with fishing gear, a cooler of food, his sleeping bag, and a tent.

"Goodbye, Ella. I'll be back in three days. I'll fish the river canyon, up in the northern part of the state. It's only a four hour drive from here. I'll be fine."

"Goodbye, honey. Have a good trip," was her usual comforting answer.

"My father would throw his hands up and go fishing sometimes when things got tough," he said. "Many times he'd come back to a nice rain, and then plant seed."

"I hope it works," she said with a kind smile.

"Bye, Dad. I'll take care of the animals," Clara said.

"Love you both. I'll send some pictures of the river."

"That would be cool. Love you too, and be careful in the canyon," she said.

I was sitting by her and noticed a pause in her voice before she said it, and I felt something odd about that moment. *I think she senses something that I don't. He's just going fishing. What could happen?* Then I started thinking about where he was going. It was a deep canyon I had heard him say. And the current was swift. I got up and went over to my master's pickup and waited for him to drop the tailgate, so I could jump in.

"No, Ace, you've got to stay home. The water is swift, and there're rattlesnakes around."

So that's why they call it the Snake River, I thought. *You better not go without me.* I jumped to try and get over the tailgate, but couldn't make it, and fell back to the ground.

"Ace, quit it, and listen to me. You can't go!"

"Dad, maybe you should let him go. Then at least you'll have a companion."

Beans was standing close by, watching things play out as usual.

"You'd better mind him. He'll be alright without you," she told me with a look.

But I couldn't stop thinking, *He shouldn't go alone.*

Clara had written in her journal about the river canyon once, after her father had taken her there. I heard the story when she read it to her mother one night, while I was lying in the kitchen.

"It was so beautiful, and nothing like I've ever seen in Nebraska before. We walked and climbed down the trail with our day packs and fishing gear. There were pines all around us, and it was quiet, except for the sound of wind through the trees. We reached the edge of the river, and, to my delight, the forest opened up to a blue, rock-strewn stream of water. When we stepped in, it was cold, and clear. We crossed it, and then Dad said we needed to climb back up the other side, to get where the fishing was good. So we did. By then, I was already tired but I made it. That was a special day."

That told me a little more about the trip my boss was about to take. I shifted positions on the floor, and my eyes didn't close.

The next two mornings, I awoke and went outside with Clara to feed the animals instead of going with Evan, wherever he was. She would give me a hard biscuit from the box by the door which was shaped like a bone. *I don't know why these are shaped like bones, but they're sure good anyway,* I thought.

Beans would get one too. "Who cares?" she replied.

She always crunched hers up in a flurry, so I would run off with mine right away. Sometimes the wolf in her would tell her mine was hers too.

I felt the long divide of space that was between Evan and me. At night, I moved from place to place to sleep a while or to listen for problems. I just had to deal with one catfight, and I prevailed.

Out in the barn one afternoon before, I'd heard my boss talking on the phone to someone in Washington. It seemed they were trying to get him to come there and testify on the farm bill I kept hearing about. *Well,* I thought to myself, *I could testify to the fact that there are too many farm cats around here, and that a t-bone steak is the best kind, since it leaves me with something to chew on, but that's about it.* This seemed much more important, though, from the looks on my boss's face.

"When is the hearing?" he asked. "August? Well, that's a pretty good time for me to come in." He started pacing a bit, and I had to move before he accidentally stepped on my foot.

"I'll book the plane tickets, and start preparing my testimony. This Congress is divided. They need to hear from a real farmer with a real good idea to solve these low corn prices. I'll present them the farm bill proposal my older and wiser brother has just devised. He knows since he's fought the same battles.

Evan started walking faster in circles on the barn floor, so I moved further away.

"I'll stay all week if I have to, and meet with those key senators to give them a piece of my mind."

About then, the black cat screamed as his foot was getting smashed by my boss's boot.

"Dang it, cat! Can't you see I'm busy?"

The cat ran out the door, and I took off after it, seeing it was needing to be straightened out some.

"Yeah, I know it might not happen unless I come," I heard as I turned the corner out the barn door.

From what I'd understood after the last few years, I think he was right. It seemed that Congress just couldn't figure out what to do to fix the problem, and even our farm was getting shaky because of it. Somebody was mucking up the water, I figured. *If I could be there, I'd sure chase them out,* I thought.

But from the looks in my boss's eyes, it wasn't going to be as easy as chasing a cat out of the barn. The system was entrenched with folks that wanted to protect their own bone, it seemed, and didn't really care about the effect it had on anyone else. I've heard of a dog-eat-dog world out there, and the thought of that turned me inside out, so I figured it was just a way of saying things could get pretty nasty sometimes.

Evan can handle it, I thought. He'd deal with about anything when I was at his side. *Maybe I give him more courage when he sees me dealing with the varmints around here,* I thought. I'm not sure it was really the people in Congress that were the problem, though, but those that were feeding them. I guessed my boss was going to have a lot to deal with in a few months.

Shifting Winds

The last night I was home without him, the wind shifted to the northwest about midnight. It was cooler then, as I lay on the front porch. Beans was on the sidewalk down in front of me and asleep, it seemed. My nose is always at work, but when he was gone, it was even more so. Quite suddenly my head turned north, while my nose started moving from side to side, taking in as much smell as I could. It was terribly faint. *Evan!* I thought.

About that time, Beans heard me stir and picked her head up. She, too, looked north intently, and I saw her nose move carefully. She stood up about the time I did. She looked at me and said, "It's him, isn't it?"

I looked back with a confirmation in my eyes of what I had just smelled, and my ears lifted.

"I think so. But it's so faint, it must be miles away," she indicated. "About a hundred and fifty," she replied after she picked up the scent some more.

"I think he's hurt," I replied.

We left at that moment, without barking to wake up Clara or anything. I followed this time, since Beans seemed to know where she was going, and the fastest way to get there. The stars were bright that night, which helped us to find our way in the dark. Beans moved confidently forward in a loping pace. It wasn't too fast that we had to break into a pant, yet fast enough to get somewhere. She set it and I followed, while I kept my nose going, and my ears lifted some.

We travelled along a wide road ditch for quite a while that night. It was pretty flat, and I could smell swampy ground to our right. Vehicles went by from time to time, and sometimes the light would flash on us. We moved a little faster when the car would brake, and we saw the bright red lights from behind. Beans would look back with a little worry on her face and a drop of her tail, like she didn't want to be noticed. I didn't worry about the tail thing since I didn't have much to work with.

About dawn, the highway led us to the river, which we drank from. I figured this wasn't the river we were headed to, since there was no canyon to be seen, and Beans sure didn't indicate that we were even close. She sat down a bit, but kept her head to west and north. I was getting hungry so I tried to eat some grass but it didn't work out.

The sun hadn't moved very far up behind us when we caught his scent again, this time a little stronger. We both jumped up and headed that way, crossing the shallow water. Suddenly we both had to swim for a few seconds, and then our feet touched ground again. I climbed up the bank and shook off for a second before I took off to catch Beans, a few paces ahead of me.

"Wait up a second," I said.

"There's no time," she replied with her tail higher now and ears forward.

The mention of time boosted me, and I was at her side, in a flash.

The valley started leaving us, and the land started turning to hills with some trees. We moved away from the road since it turned too far west, away from where our noses were pointing. We crossed fences and went by herds of cattle grazing. There were a few deep ravines we went down and back up, with trees all around. I wondered if this was it but the stream was too small, and the scent still too faint. So I kept following Beans and the scent. Beans never even took the time to mark the trail like she usually did.

"Keep moving, Ace. We've got to get there soon."

"I'm with you, girl. Find the quickest route for us."

I sensed more drive and more courage in her, by the way she moved and the way her head stayed up, with eyes fixed on the horizon. A flush of pride came over me, and then it was gone as we raced forward.

The trees left us as we started to climb what looked like grass-covered dunes of sand. My feet slipped in it some, and a few times I stepped on a cactus that poked in my pad. Quickly, I sat down and pulled it out with lips pulled back, out of the way. Then I lunged forward to catch up and saw Beans had the same problem. I looked back at her, holding her rear foot up and reaching back to pull out one of those nasty things. *Somebody oughta outlaw cactus plants,* I thought.

Beans was soon at my side, saying little, and smelling the way forward with me. Sometimes the scent was lost to one of us so the other took over. We worked together as a team, while I worried, separately, about the fate of our boss.

The day waned, and the sun was now in front of us. Wincing as it blinded me, I stumbled over a bush and ran into a dense clump of grass taller than me. For a little while I moved off to the right of Beans so she could block the sun with her body. It worked well. Soon, it was just a half round orange ball, like the rubber one my boss used to throw down the lane for me to fetch. This one, all of a sudden, seemed to be moving too fast for me to catch before it was gone.

Twilight is a hard time to see, even for a dog. Things get mixed up in shadows, and surroundings seem different. This didn't bother Beans much. She seemed to be used to traveling in the dark, and I counted on her wisdom as to what was the best route around obstacles in our way. At one point, we saw the lights of a city off to our right. Beans began to veer left, further than I would have. I didn't complain - just kept at her side. Soon the lights started dimming, and she moved back closer to the route my nose said to follow. It was strong now, and I sensed we were getting close. I could see a long line of trees ahead of us on the horizon. They looked black and dense, like a wall we were about to have to cross. But before that, we came across a highway. It was a black road, on a curve that wound down to our left. I could see right a long ways, and nothing was coming. To our left we heard the sound of a truck, but no lights yet.

"Let's go," Beans said.

"Gotcha," I replied as I touched down on the hard pavement.

About that second, the headlights hit us full on. I saw the reflection of them in Beans' eyes as she looked toward them. We lunged forward as the truck slammed on its brakes. Crossing the ditch, I squirmed under the bottom wire of the fence while she stepped over, between the upper wires. I heard a yelp, as a shred of fur came off her while she pushed through, hardly slowing down. The pickup backed up and turned its lights into a lane and onto a gate as I looked back. Somebody jumped out from the passenger seat and threw it open. There was a roar of the diesel engine as it took off after us. Beans was ahead of me just a little, and she dropped over the edge of a dune. As I looked back to see how close they were, a clump of grass came my way and knocked me flat down. In an instant, they were on me, with the driver jumping out to grab me by the scruff. I yelped! *Where's Beans when I really need her most?* I thought. Remembering that night when I was little, and the men took me out of the back of the SUV. I shook the same though now I was a grown dog.

The big man picked me up easily. Lucky for him he had gloved hands, as my incisors went into them. He almost dropped me. I was trembling even more now. It was happening so fast.

"What are you doing, running out in cow country?" he said.

This can't be happening now, I thought to myself, as I looked ahead and towards where we thought our boss was.

"That's not much of an Australian shepherd, is it?" the other guy said.

It's not the size of the tiger, but the size of the fight in the tiger, I thought as he opened a cage door in the back of his truck.

"We don't need any more dogs chasing our calves," he said.

In the pen to my right, a tall, thin greyhound snarled at me, and scratched at the wire mesh between us.

"What are you doing out here in the middle of the night?" it said. "You're lucky you weren't a coyote, or I would have chased you down, and they would have shot you."

Shivering, I slunk down and looked out the back door of the cage. *I'm sunk now.*

The pickup started moving again, turning back the way it came. About that time, I saw Beans come running up and by the truck.

Again, the brakes slammed, and the two men jumped out.

"Get him!" the man said, like he was talking to one of his dogs but actually his partner.

Her, I thought, though there wasn't much time to think.

Beans flew by the back of the pickup with two men chasing her.

"You stinkin' dog, I'll catch you!" he shouted.

I was whining in the box. *There's got to be a way out of this. We can't be stopped right now.*

After about two times around, the men were starting to huff, in between their yelling at Beans and each other. I would have thought that one would stop and go the other way to catch her in a trap but sometimes humans get wrapped up in the moment and just aren't all that smart. Beans was ahead enough to stop and jump up at the door of the cage. She hit the quick release bar with her paw. It was built that way, so when they saw a coyote they could let the greyhounds out fast. I used it to my advantage and exited fast.

I thought, *Funny thing, this dog knowing how they work,* as I jumped to the ground, wired like a spring, with my feet moving as they hit. We were off in the night in a flash, away from the pickup lights; me shaking off my trembling. *That could have been really bad.* I heard the two doors slam and soon saw the truck lights circling around us. We jumped over the dune and were gone.

"That was close," I said.

"Darn close. I'm never going to a pound again," Beans replied.

"I don't think they had the pound in mind for you," I replied, thinking of the snarling greyhound, and guns in the rack of the back window of the pickup cab.

It wasn't long before we reached the tree line. I readied to bound through it, when suddenly Beans stopped, and I ran into her butt.

"Could you give me a little more warning next time?" I said as I picked myself up.

"Next time," she said, "There's a cliff here, just a few feet away."

I guess that hitting the butt end of her wasn't so bad.

Both of us headed up the tree line where a ridge had formed. I never saw a place we could go down but really I couldn't see much. All the while, the scent got stronger.

"This must be the canyon he's in," I said.

"It is!" she replied with a confident swing of her tail.

After a while of this, we both sat down and looked over the cliff edge. My paws actually hung down over the rocks, as the air of the canyon came swooping up to my nose. I smelled pine trees, water, dusty chalk rock, and a deer. Behind me, I could hear the sound of a coyote pack and thought, *I'm glad not to be one of those kinds of dogs.* Beans ignored them and kept her nose to the canyon. She stood and started moving up the ridge line again. His scent was getting stronger all the time, and I lunged ahead of her. I had it now, and I wasn't going to let it go.

We made our way between the trees and rocks, along the edge a little further. Beans stopped about the same time I did. Simultaneously I detected the scent of something I'd never smelled before. When I heard the bloodcurdling scream, I knew it was a mountain lion, like my mother had told me stories about.

I reactively scrunched down a little, right on the ledge. A wave of powerful Evan scent struck me, and I knew we had found him. But the cliff was high, and the canyon deep. A stone fell off the side, as I shifted my head down looking into the depths. It rattled and bounced, getting quieter, and soon it was gone. Then I heard a moan from my boss. It was a sound I had never heard from him before. The hair stood up on my back with these two events shocking my brain, like an electric fence I'd mistakenly touched. *He's hurt bad. I've got to get down there quick, and be at his side. I should've gone with him. I gotta learn to jump over that tailgate.*

"Get out of here, you beast," I heard Evan whisper weakly.

A rock clunked on the ground, while I heard my boss's hand fall on the chalky wall, and the lion hissed and snarled some more.

It was our turn to make some noise, and I started barking with all my might. Beans did too, which she only did when things were serious. We sounded off the night, yet I could easily hear the mountain lion scream right through it.

"Ace, is that you? And Beans!"

The sound echoed in the canyon, and it was real good to hear him say our names. But he wasn't out of the woods. I knew he was hurt from the scent of his blood rising to us, and the lion was still pacing back and forth. We raced along the canyon edge looking for a way down but there wasn't one. We kept barking as we ran, hoping it would be enough to keep the predator away from our Evan. *There's no one to go find in twenty miles. It's all up to us.*

* * * * *

The minutes turned to hours as we waited for the sun to rise behind our backs and light the way. We had the grass beaten down for a hundred yards along the ridge, and my feet hurt. They were cut and pierced, and one pad felt like it was coming off. Beans stayed intent, and I tried to not run into her as our paths crossed along the trail we had made. A mistake would have meant disaster. As the sun came up, I soon saw the outline of the beast between the river and the canyon wall. It was bigger than the two of us combined by thirty pounds, I bet.

Then, as the sun allowed us to see straight down, I spotted him right against the cliff. His head was lower than his body. One leg was pinched between the wall and a boulder that was resting on the floor of the canyon. It was holding in him that position. I could see a piece of white sticking through his jeans, and this I knew was real bone. Red, like the raw meat we get once in a while, surrounded the bone. I shivered and squirmed as Beans kept pacing, looking for a place to get down.

"You go ahead up the ridge and look for a place," I said. "I'll hold off the lion till you do."

"It's a plan", she said, and she bounded forward.

Knowing my task, I barked even louder as I ran back and forth. A few rocks fell off the edge in my frenzy, which seemed to scare the beast some, keeping it off balance. Now I could see the situation. My boss was just out of reach of the lion. Scrapes and tracks told the story of the animal coming close to the man with a broken leg. That must have been so appealing to a hungry cat, far larger than any creature I had ever dealt with, even in my dreams.

I could now see his pocket tool lying close to him - the shiny steel flashed in the sun. And I saw the part sticking out that he used to saw small tree limbs off with. But there were no limbs around, other than his.

He was getting ready to saw his own leg off! I thought. My stomach felt like the night in the car when I was a pup. *It could have been another owner of the farm with a missing leg!* More so, I worried how desperate my boss had been. At that point, I realized Evan's great will to survive. *How powerful it must be for him, to go to the lengths he was planning. If he can do that, then I can at least be brave enough save him.*

About then, Beans came running out of the trees to my left below, along the water.

She wasn't far from the cat, and I realized the fight was on - and without me.

Clara's Nightmare

Clara went to bed that night expecting her father to be home late, and that she would see him in the morning. He had gone fishing to the river canyon many times before and would drive home only after fishing most of the day. But this night, though she tried to go to sleep right away, she couldn't. She rolled a few times and adjusted her pillow. Things in her mind just wouldn't settle.

I've got that same feeling I had when Dad fell into a hole on the four-wheeler, and hurt himself. But nothing's wrong. His headlights will shine on the ceiling soon when he comes in the driveway, she thought. *This time it's my mind racing around in a panic, not me.*

About midnight, she went to sleep. No light had entered her bedroom. The dream she had that night was filled with darkness. It turned into a nightmare when she visualized her father dead, lying on the ground, while the sheriff handed her mother papers on the farm foreclosure at the porch door.

She woke up in a start. Daylight filled her room, and it was quiet. Clara looked at her phone, and it was eight o'clock. *Weather forecast, sunny with a good chance of thunderstorms late in the afternoon,* she read. She walked to her parents' room and peered around the door but saw only her mother in the bed. Walking the wide, creaking stairway to the living room, and on to the kitchen, she found no one. Clara went to the front porch, in case he was drinking his coffee there with the dogs at his side, like on so many mornings.

Nothing. No dogs. No Dad. She folded her arms, looked out, and shivered a little. Then it struck her like a long-ago premonition that she had just realized. *He's in trouble! He's hurt! Where are the dogs? Are they out hunting?* Something stirred deep inside. She sat down with her arms still folded and rocked back and forth, thinking. *They went to find him. That's it!*

She raced inside and upstairs to wake her mother. "He's not home! The dogs are gone! I've got a terrible feeling!"

They left ten minutes later without even feeding any of the animals. On the way, they called Jamie to tell him the situation. He calculated the time it would take for the dogs to reach their father if they happened to take a straight course. He understood their capacity and their loyalty to a master. *It just could be,* he thought. *They could get there in twenty-four hours if they traveled six miles an hour. They might already be there. But what's happened to my father?*

The drive seemed to go on forever, on the paved road that led up the long valley, into the grass-covered sand dunes of northern Nebraska. To the west, a cloud bank had developed.

"It's going to rain and storm this afternoon, and you know how scared Ace is of the thunder," Clara told her mother.

"I'm more worried about your father right now," Ella replied, as she gripped the wheel with both hands. "But he's resourceful, and I think he'll be all right. Maybe his pickup just broke down. Those darn dogs taking off right, now, too."

Clara put her head down. *But that's not what the dream told me,* she thought. *How will we or the farm ever get along without him? I'm not ready for that. Will there even be a farm left to take care of?*

About that time, there was a bang, and the pickup swerved to the left, crossing the center line. Ella pulled left on the wheel and stepped on the brake. The pickup turned right as they skidded into a lane with a fence gate ahead of them.

"It's a tire! We've blown a tire, Clara!"

I knew Dad should have put on a new set sooner, but he kept saying that times are tough, she thought.

"I've got it, I think," Clara responded, as she grabbed the handle of the door and swung herself out.

On her side of the truck, she saw the collapsed, worn-down tire.

"I can change it!" she said. "Dad taught me how when we blew one on the trailer one day."

Clara swung into action, leaning the back of the seat forward to get the jack and kit out.

"I'll get the tire out of the truck," Ella said, as she climbed up into the box and moved a handyman jack, a coil of rope, and some other junk, out of the way.

A farmer's pickup is always so messy, Clara thought. *Always too much stuff.*

"Just a minute, I need to set the emergency brake."

As she rounded the front fender of the pickup to get there, she noticed the tuft of grey and black hair on the barbed wire by the fence gate.

"That's from Beans!" she yelled. "We've found their trail, I bet. Let's open the gate and follow the track road towards the canyon." *If they made it this far, I bet they have found him. But is he okay?*

Broken Bones

Beans didn't hesitate. I froze in my tracks for a moment, watching it play out. The beast showed no sign of fear, facing my sidekick, tail switching, and head down a little. Its intent eyes seemed to burn right into her. About the time she reached the lion, barking as hard as I've ever heard, she took a hard right. The cat's swipe missed her by inches, as it swung around to stay head on with her opponent. I saw all five claws. Beans circled and then rolled back the other way, keeping the cat off balance.

Now! I thought, as the stones flew under my feet, some of them dropping and hitting Evan. I looked down but he didn't move, and his eyes weren't open. *We're too late.* As I raced along the canyon ridge, I looked for the place where Beans found her way down. Soon I found the little ravine between the trees and walls. I headed down as fast as I could, over rocks and downed limbs. Jumping from the trunk of a fallen tree, I hit the steep ground and started rolling down the washout. When I stopped, I was at the bottom and could hear the fight heading further down the canyon stream. I took off, and made my way through the tall grass. The scream of the cat hit me, and another burst of energy drove me on.

Beans was continuing her maneuvers we had practiced on the snake a year or so back. The cat was tiring, I noticed, but not giving in. Just as I got there, she stopped instead of turning.

This caught Beans off guard, and the cat had her. She grabbed her by the neck and started shaking Beans, like I would with an intruding cat in the barn. The beast seemed to have summoned new energy, upon getting hold of my sidekick. Suddenly, she let go, and Beans flew against the canyon wall, and landed in a heap. She didn't get up like I expected her to. *Maybe she hit her head, and it's over,* I thought in a flash, while thinking of Rosy. *Two down and one left -tigers and fights.*

The mountain lion seemed to discount me and headed for Evan again. I could see the trail she had paced in an oval around the lower side of the boulder. She began jumping and clawing at the rocks to try and reach him, becoming even more incensed. As she made another lunge at my boss's arm hanging down, she drew blood, and then slid back down. *By damn, I'm not going to let it happen, even if he is dead!*

She seemed oblivious to me at that moment. I ran toward her and latched on to her tail, about six inches from the end. I bit down as hard as I could, and locked my jaws on like a pit bull. *See how this feels!* She screamed and swung around to reach me but that just caused me to swoop around. Soon she was chasing her own tail. Pretty soon I was swinging around like I've seen kids do on the swing rides when the carnival comes to town. It was getting to be quite a ride. It was a good thing my opponent was always right in front of me. She kept turning, and swung me through some cactus plants. The thorns stuck into me through my fur, and I winced but held on, biting down harder. This angered the cat even more. About the last swing around, I noticed Beans move. *She's alive!*

In a few seconds, she stood up and shook herself. *Getting the cobwebs out of her head,* I thought. I felt a rush of pride hit when Beans came at the cat again, with fury now. I let go so I could help better and said, "Grab her front leg!"

I heard the crunch of bone, like when Beans tried to eat an old steak bone. This was followed by a scream from the cat like no other. She lunged at Beans but faltered when she tried to step on the leg. Beans let go and backed up. I was on the other side, between Evan and the cat.

"You've broken it," she cried to us, sounding like a kitten.

"Go lick your wounds and leave us alone," Beans said after spitting out some hair in her mouth.

"I'll leave you for another day. Don't ever come back here," warned the lion.

Maybe not, I thought. *This is her domain, and we probably don't belong here. We'd be coming at our own risk, because I know cats have to eat too.*

The cat limped off down the canyon, as we watched and thought of what had just taken place.

About then, lightning hit a tree not far up the canyon. The bolt lit up the sky that had gone dim from the dark clouds over head. I cringed, and shivered a bit, but this time because it felt like I had hit an electric fence again. I wanted to run and hide in the barn. I turned to Evan for reassurance in these cases but he still wasn't moving.

Disaster and Despair

The tire, though low, had enough air in it to hold the truck up. Clara opened the gate as Ella jumped in the driver's seat. She jammed it into gear, and Clara climbed in, leaving the gate open. *I hope no cows get out on the road,* she thought.

They followed the sand trail up and around the dunes. It was soft in places, and the loose sand made them sink and spin out. "Put it in four wheel drive, Mom!" she said.

"Done." Ella pulled back the lever on the floor of the old truck.

The gear ground a bit, and then the pickup lurched forward up the trail. Soon the tree line was in sight again.

"We must be getting close, Mom!"

"I'll take the trail to the left - it seems the most used," she said.

I hope she's right, Clara thought.

Soon they reached the canyon. They both jumped out of the truck and looked down over the precipice. There we were, in the midst of the thunder and lightning. It was beginning to rain.

"Mom, there must be a way down," Clara said. "Let's go that way," she said.

Ella ran after her.

"Stay there, Mom! We might need something out of the truck!" she yelled back.

"Be careful! Don't you fall too, Clara!"

* * * * *

I heard stones rattling down on us, and then the rain came pouring down.

Clara soon reached us, and I leaned up against her leg for a second. Beans was in front of her wagging her tail with her tongue out. But she immediately turned back to our boss. I left her leg as fast as I had gotten to it and followed.

What happens if this valley starts flooding, I thought.

There wasn't much time to think, and the rain hitting Clara in the face made everything more difficult.

Beans was on one side of the boulder near my boss's foot, and I was on the other side, looking up at his limp arms. We both were scrambling to reach him but neither of us had the ability to climb that far. Clara was soon in front of us, battling to grab a hand hold in the wall. She reached her father and touched his head and then his neck with her other hand.

"He's cold!" she yelled. "We've got to get him out of here!"

She slid back down and sized up the situation. Water poured off the canyon wall, washing dirt out from under Evan - but he was still stuck.

Clara yelled back to Ella, "The boulder is big but I think if we can move it a little, his leg will get freed!"

I looked at the size of the rock, and looked at Beans. There was no way we were going to move that rock but then I had a thought. "Let's start digging around it!"

I motioned to Beans who was immediately at my side, and we began tearing away at the soft rock. The dirt flew into the rain and washed down the canyon.

Ella yelled down, "What can I get you to help? There's a handyman jack in the back."

I had seen Evan pick up an old wagon with this jack. It was tall, and had a ratchet mechanism that would let him lift all kinds of things pretty easily, higher than my head.

"That might work—we could lay it sideways and try to push the rock away from the wall," Clara yelled over the thunderous rain.

"I'll tie it onto that rope I saw in there, and lower over the edge!" Ella replied.

The jack was heavy and cumbersome, I knew, but I figured she could lift it. Soon, I saw the jack coming over the edge with a blue rope tied to it. The jack kept coming. I couldn't see Ella but I knew she had to be hanging onto the rope. It stopped suddenly when it hit a ledge and rested on it. The rope went limp.

"Lift it up and down!" Clara yelled.

It moved some, and soon a chunk of rock broke off the wall. It flew down and narrowly missed Evan's head. I dodged it as it rolled by me. But the jack was free and was reaching the top of the boulder.

"Stop!" Clara yelled, and the jack hung motionless right above us. Clara went to the other side and found another handhold. She labored and found a foothold. Soon she was standing on the top of the boulder, above her father.

I saw her shivering there and wondered. *Is this hopeless? Is it just too bad of a situation? We're going to lose my boss, my best friend, and everything he cares for.*

Clara seemed undeterred and grabbed the jack, then untied the rope. *She's as determined as he is,* I thought. I watched her place the foot of it against the canyon wall and the lift piece on a sharp edge of the boulder. The long handle stood upright in front of her.

Beans was still digging but Clara yelled at her to "Get away!" so she obediently did.

Clara started pumping the jack handle. I heard one click, then two, then another. She was grimacing now, and I saw the slight bulge of her arm muscle, and she pushed on the handle. I noticed the boulder move just a little. I hoped for another click, but didn't hear one. Some stones slid off the top of the boulder, and Beans dodged them.

"I can't get it but it moved a little!" she yelled up to her mom. "There's only room for one of us on the top of this rock, and I don't think you will even be able to climb up here!"

Clara stood up and looked out over the rising stream. I saw the look of despair on her face. If tears were coming down, I couldn't tell, as the sky seemed to be crying with her.

Suddenly she turned. "Throw me the other end of the rope, Mom!"

It slid down and coiled up on her father's waist and chest. She grabbed the end and tied a big loop. Then she laid it around the top of the boulder. She coiled up the rest of it and cast it at us.

I was starting to get it.

"Grab hold, Beans!" I said.

"Finally! A chance to use my tugging skills!" Beans said, and sunk her teeth into the end of the rope.

I grabbed on a little ahead of her, and we dug in, tugging as hard as we could. But the rock wouldn't move anymore. I saw Clara collapse to her knees, her face crumpled.

Ella stood at the top of the cliff, holding the phone to her ear. "So, build a four-point harness from a piece of the rope? Beans can pull better going forward, Jamie says," she yelled. "Then find a can of spray in the truck, and oil the jack pins, so there's less friction? Will do! Make sure the knots are good, he says!"

She relayed this to Clara, with more confidence reflecting in her voice. Ella went to find a can of lubricant while Clara traversed down the rock and wall. She took out her pocket tool and cut a length of rope.

"Jamie once showed me how to do this. I've got to remember," she said.

Beans stood like the stone she was being asked to pull while Clara put the harness together.

I went to check Evan. *Still no movement.*

There is something mighty about a sled dog's willingness to pull. This was no exception as her Husky breeding came out. I felt the rope behind me stretch and surge as I waited for another click. My little effort seemed nothing compared to what I felt. Beans dug in with her claws fully out, and yanked terribly hard. I think I heard a tendon snap in her leg, and a whine, but there was no reduction in pull. Clara screamed in the agony of her effort.

Then I heard the clicks.

On the third one, I saw Evan's body slide down the soft dirt to the bottom, with his leg dangling behind.

I dropped on my paws for a second, as he came to rest close to us, and I released the rope. Everything about him seemed gone and empty.

The river had doubled in size about the time it stopped raining, but there was still room between the wall and the water. We three stood there over Evan's body.

I could see Ella on her cell phone, and soon I heard the *chop, chop* of what I had come to know as a helicopter. Evan would exclaim, "Somebody's real sick," as he looked into the sky on the farm as one went over with a red marking on the side. This one came over the bank with a rush of wind and noise. I put my head down, and I saw Bean's ears flutter around. A long cable with a basket dropped down with a man standing in it. He had a special suit on and all kinds of gear on him, with a stethoscope around his neck. The shiny metal circle touched Evan's arm as the things went into the man's ears.

He paused and stood back up. "I'm sorry, there is no pulse," he said.

Clara looked up toward her mom, and with the most desperate, forlorn look on her face I've ever seen, shook her head sideways.

"Check him again," Ella screamed back, standing in one place yet bouncing up and down, like she was doing a prayer dance or something.

The man went back down on his knee, and put the tool to Evan's heart again but this time for longer. He stood up, and while shaking his head sideways in the blasting wind, yelled, "There's still none."

I couldn't watch her anymore but I did see her fall to her knees, looking upward in the sky, screaming, and a wailing sound like I've never heard before. They had been as close as my master and I had been. *Probably even closer given they came from the same family.* The hurt I felt seemed even worse with this thought. It was like a wound on top of a wound that hadn't even started to heal yet. I first whined, then put my nose to the sky and howled. Maybe something out there would hear.

Flying Beyond the Earth

The storm had subsided, but the rain from tired, glistening eyes still streamed down Clara's face. Beans obediently sat down beside her and watched. The man went around and reached low to pick Evan up under his shoulders. Clara, still able, grabbed his broken leg and moved it along with him. The man slid his front into the basket, then came around and gently lifted his legs in as well. The wind from the blades was hitting us all in sharp blasts. Time seemed to stop in a way. I could see what was about to happen just as the man motioned with a twirling finger at the helicopter pilot.

The basket started lifting off the ground.

It struck me at that moment that I had to go with him. I leaped forward before anyone could stop me. Jumping higher than I ever had before, I grabbed the edge of the basket with my front feet as it went up, and hooked one of my back feet over the edge too. Soon I was sitting on Evan's chest as we sailed into the sky in the little basket.

I'm not sure if the pilot saw me, though I didn't care. Below, I saw the man's look of shock as we rose. Clara's eyes were squeezed closed. Bean's tail was wagging, though, which gave me some hope.

We flew by Ella. She stood there looking up at me, with her long hair and checkered blouse blowing in the torrent of wind. Soon we were high over the trees, headed towards the line of blue, far to the east. Behind me was the orange glow of the ball, just above the clear horizon. My chest that had been pounding so hard started to settle down. I lay down with the wind rushing by me and my boss. I smelled all kinds of things.

Home.

The mountain lion.

Pine trees.

Prairie grass.

Sage.

Cattle.

Rain.

Sulfur from the lightning.

Yet the overpowering smell was of Evan - the scent I'd lived for all the time on the farm. The human I'd given my heart and soul to all these years. It gave me solace, that at least he was here, and I was with him still. Each morning we met for all these years, excitement came over me when I first caught his scent. But now his scent was somewhat different. It had blood, pain, heavy sweat, and stress partly covering the good smell he carried. And there was something else. The smell I picked up when I walked by Rosy on her last day.

My other sense, though, said, "Don't give up." Lying down on him, I pressed my chest tight against him. My two beat-up paws were around his head, and I started licking his face. I could feel my heart pound against his body. We were high now. I could see the lights of the city we had skirted the night before, ahead of the dark blue cloud line. It was just me and my Evan dangling far below the blades cutting the evening sky.

Something came over me, and I don't even know now what it was. I kept licking him. I licked his neck, and his chest that was exposed above his shirt. I licked his face the most. My mother had taught me the power of my tongue to heal a wound, so I used her advice, even though this was far beyond anything I'd ever tried to heal on myself. The sound somehow went away, and it grew quiet. We were still flying somewhere, with the noise of the helicopter and the wind all around. I didn't know where we were going.

A powerful connection formed between us - and between the two of us and something else.

I'm not sure what it was but it was there.

Dogs were supposed to die before their masters do. I'd always been good with that. This scene wasn't right.

But we dogs have strong hearts. ... And I sensed some of my heart leaving and rushing into him.

Evan's eyes opened right before we landed, and I collapsed at his side in the basket. With my head resting near his, my eyes looked upon his face and the sky all at once.

* * * * *

We set down on a red square cross on the pavement.

They about had to peel me away from him. *I'm not leaving, you don't understand, he is the one I love,* I thought. I gave in, though, since I really had no choice. I figured the people vets had mothers who taught them some things too. That feeling I'd had was gone now, like it wasn't needed anymore. I spun around and danced in circles on the pavement, like I had just caught something. But I wasn't that surprised, given the feeling that had rushed over me just minutes before. And then I sat obediently, at his side with my eyes on only him.

A hand tugged on my collar, and I followed it.

"He has a pulse!" the person said after kneeling down with the shiny steel instrument again.

He didn't have to tell me. I already knew.

My boss was lifted onto a stretcher and wheeled toward the hospital big door. I pulled on my collar hard, broke loose from the person holding me, and lunged for Evan. We met at the door. Maybe it was the noise of the person yelling at me to stop but Evan's eyes opened, and he saw me.

"Ace," he said weakly.

Don't worry. I'm here, Evan.

His hand fell off the side of the stretcher, and he reached out and stroked my fur. The medic crew stopped, and all became quiet for a moment again. I saw his eyes glisten, and a tear roll down his cheek. Then one said, "We've got to go," and they wheeled him in while I stood there. There were more tears in his eyes when I looked up, as the team followed Evan through the door.

It wasn't long, and the pickup showed up with Beans in the back - her head reaching out over the side. Clara and her mom jumped out. Beans just leaped, and soon they were all at my side.

"They called and told me he's alive!" Ella said.

"Beans, we saved him," I said.

Beans just stood there at attention, her tail wagging high, and her tongue hanging out.

The helicopter medic, who had helped Evan into the stretcher at the canyon, had come along too. "I can't believe it," he said to a doctor who was still outside. "He was dead."

The doctor looked down at the ground for a moment, and was quiet.

"Sometimes things happen that we just can't explain. This is what we call a miracle. I think that, for all we know, there is a lot more to life that we just don't know about," he said with a soft smile on his face.

That had me looking down at the ground. I knew raccoons and badgers, cows and squirrels. I knew all that my mom had taught me. I know this story. Myself, I thought I knew. Instinctual knowledge was buried deep into my brain. *Yet I don't know how what had just happened could have happened.*

That's the last I saw of Evan for quite a while. Although, at that point, I was okay with that. Flying in the sky, with all that had taken place, and then being able to see the bigness of it all, had changed me.

I feel a little closer to the stars right now, I thought, *like I've accomplished what I set out to do. I'm not that big of a deal but the farm sure is to me. I'm just a little farm dog, trying to do his best. If something happens to me, well, so be it. I'll be alright out there.*

Fortitude and Fortune

Ella brought Evan home, while Clara stayed with us on the farm. Beans and I raced around the pickup to his side. We sat quickly, with tails sweeping the lawn by the driveway. I looked up with the brightest of eyes. *What's he going to be like? I sure hope he can walk with us.* I looked around to make sure no cats would come around and trip him up.

"Hi, Ace, you good boy," he said. "And Beans, you good girl! I love you both."

Well, I knew from the sound of his voice he was sure glad to see us. About that time Beans heard something in the trees and looked around. She turned right back to Evan though. Then Clara came in between us to greet him. And Jamie came out of the barn and trotted over to us too. *We're all here now. All together.* I caught a glimpse of two cats walking up on the porch. *I think they're all happy too. Maybe I'll give them a break today.*

It was late summer when I saw Evan walk out of the house with his cane, stop at the door, and kiss Ella goodbye. I could see the concern on her face as their hands slipped away from each other. Clara had just loaded his suitcase in the car, and stood beside me. Beans was out on the front porch standing watch. I, too, had begun to limp, just like my boss did now.

"Give 'em hell in Washington," Ella said.

"I won't give them hell; I'll just tell them the truth. They'll think that is hell," he replied.

My tail swept the sidewalk as I listened.

Give 'em a good bite for me, I thought.

"Bye, Dad, love you. Bring me a little something cool, if you think about it," Clara said.

"Sure thing." *Maybe a pretty hand mirror from the Union Station shops,* he thought.

"Don't forget to take your medicine," Ella said again, and he smiled in return.

* * * * *

Jamie, who lived closer, had gone to the hearings to watch his dad. Later I heard him tell Ella and Clara all about it. He said his father looked good in his new suit, as he walked up to the center chair of the hearing room. He leaned his cane on the table in front of him, laid his papers in front of the microphone, and then took his seat in the dark brown leather swivel chair.

"Sir, please give us your full name and where you're from for the record," the senator stated. "Then you may begin."

Jamie said he was surprised Evan hadn't given them his carefully prepared speech that day, as he had planned. Instead he told them stories about the history of his farm, and the families who had lived there. He told them about Jessie and Nancy, and Homer and Donald, and the windstorm. He told them about the droughts and the crops. He talked of the evening skies and the morning sunrise from the front porch. He told them about his neighbors and their families who worked so hard. He talked about the small towns and their value to society.

"I live in a place that grows corn and soybeans. In the past it has raised everything from hogs and cattle, to chickens and horses. Over its hundred year history it has grown oats and alfalfa, wheat and millet. But the most important thing it has grown was good children. I can attest to that with my fine son Jamie actually in the audience."

"This farm has seen its full share of weather too. Droughts and floods, windstorms and arctic blizzards have all spread over the place. Myself, and the generations of predecessors, have all experienced them. Yes, there was suffering involved. Weather is something we can't control. So we try and deal with what we can control. That is called farming. You here are legislators. And you have offered your service, been elected by citizens, and now positioned yourselves to do good things."

"Today I will offer you testimony, and a plan that will help you manage the one thing that you have the ability to affect. It's the one thing, other than the weather that farmers deal with and worry about, more than anything else. They must live by it. That's the market. I ask you to consider this plan, and understand its potential to improve the lives of the thousands - no millions - who will be affected by what you decide to do with it today. For when they elected you, the people have given you great power. I trust that you will use it most wisely, with the future of our great nation in mind."

Jamie said Evan finished, then laid down his speech on the table and asked that it be put in the record.

"So be it," the senator said. "Now tell me about your cane, and the accident I heard you had not long ago. They said you about died in a canyon."

Evan leaned back in his chair and relaxed just a little.

"You're incorrect, sir. I did die in the canyon."

The senator, with a balding head and bright red tie, leaned forward in his chair, and looked over his reading glasses at Evan.

"So tell me about that."

Evan paused a long time, while looking down at the table in front of him. Jamie said it became dead quiet in the hearing room. The he picked up his head, looked outward a moment and redirected his focus to the committee members.

"It was a day when I just needed to get away from it all. It had been so dry but we had everything planted. Then the market decided there was going to be a good crop and prices began collapsing. I could hardly watch what was happening day by day. So I went to a favorite fishing place I go. We all have them, don't we? A place where we can escape to - a respite. You all know. I was alone, partly by choice, even though I knew the canyon was an isolated and arduous place to climb down into, fish, and then return out of. I guess that's kind of like life, isn't it?" he said. Jamie told us there was a bit of uncomfortable shifting going on in the room, with everyone at full attention.

"I made it into the canyon fine. I didn't see any rattlesnakes on the way down. The trail is steep but ends at a whirling pool of water where the fishing is usually good. Sure enough I caught a trout on the second cast. I was carrying just a fishing vest with my gear. I always carry a good pocket tool that has a knife, pliers to pull hooks out, and a small but very sharp wood saw. I guess you could call it my survival equipment."

"The only risk I felt was in making the right choices in each move, step by step, rock by rock, through the blue-green streaming water. When it got too deep, or the flow too powerful, I went to the side and climbed up the bank. There it wasn't much easier; obstacles of downed trees, brush, and areas of poison ivy. But I always knew I'd find a way through. Then I'd slip down the bank, back into the water, and fish some more. I worked my way up the stream all afternoon, stopping only once to eat a sandwich that I'd kept in a pocket at the back of my vest. It was sunny and comfortable on the bank I chose, so I laid back, blocked the sun with my cowboy hat, and took a nap. I knew I was close enough to the stream that there wouldn't be any snakes, so I felt safe."

"Something stirred me a little while later. I'm not sure I even heard anything but something woke me. I tipped my hat up, as I sat forward and looked around. There was nothing except the beautiful sound of the stream flowing in front of me, and birds busily singing everywhere. Yet I felt something was there; a presence watching me. I shrugged it off and went fishing some more. It was pretty good, and I caught quite a few. Other than one that looked too injured to return to the water, I released them all. This one I put in by back pouch wrapped in some water grass, thinking I would cook it later for supper. All the time that afternoon I felt I was being followed."

"Towards evening I had reached an area with steep canyon terrain on both sides. I knew that the falls were ahead a short way, and there I could take a trail out to walk back to camp. I began a cast with my fly rod, and looked back to make sure I wouldn't snag a tree branch on the backward reach. That's when I saw it."

"Maybe the mountain lion was waiting for the perfect time to attack. I figure it knew the canyon better than I did, and had cornered other prey there, where there was no escape upwards, and none forwards due to the waterfalls. I had checked my options and figured this all out pretty quickly. I thought to myself how absurd this was. A day of escape from life turns into another effort to get away from the beast" Jamie said he looked down again and got quiet.

"What did you do then?" the senator asked, bringing Evan back, it seemed.

"I'm sorry. Well, lots of thoughts can go through a person's mind in a flash. Escape was certainly one of my thoughts here. I decided that the rock wall beside me had a few handholds, and maybe I could get up it, though I bet it was a hundred feet to the top. As the cat came at me, I grabbed one of them and made it up to the top of a huge, split off stone that was resting on the bottom of the canyon, and leaning out a little. I suppose I was fifteen feet above the ground. I got a good look at the cat as it reached the rock, and paced around it. I surmised it was a female, and about 120 pounds. She put her paws up on the rock and looked for a way up, swishing her tail. I thought that she just might find a way up. So I started looking for another hand hold and way to climb the wall. I'd practiced this at a rock climbing place in the city with Jamie one time, but never thought I'd need it to escape a predator like this. I told myself I was okay and this was just another hurdle to climb."

"Then I calculated a possible route up the wall. There were lots of footholds, though far apart. The rock was soft sandstone, and sometimes it would break off when you grabbed at a place. I got up about another twenty feet, and suddenly had a bird's eye view of my situation. The mountain lion was still pacing, with a quicker motion. From time to time she made a jump and scramble, to try and get to the top of the rock, but slid back each time. I thought that if I did it, she could do it too."

"The next few moves looked pretty risky. What was I to do though? I didn't see any other option. When I grabbed hold with my left hand, and stepped to the next toe hold, both gave way at once. I started sliding and falling downwards, even though I clawed for anything to stop me. I landed right in the crevasse of the big rock. My leg wedged into it, while the rest of my body fell off to the side. I heard the bone snap the same time as my fall stopped. My arms dangled down below my head, which hit a rock, dazing me."

"Oh, my God," the senator gasped.

"I came-to with the cat scratching my arm as it jumped at me. I quickly pulled my arms up to my chest. There was searing pain in my right leg. I lifted myself up as best I could, and saw the leg stuck between the wall and the rock. *In the classical sense,* I thought, and I fell back, looking up into the deep blue evening sky. I wondered if my salvation was out there."

"The blood was rushing to my head, hanging in that position, and it was difficult to think. To keep my arms up, I locked my thumbs under my belt. I couldn't see the cat anymore. I could just hear her move about below me, hissing at times. I think I was passing out for moments at a time. The pain kept me awake mostly though."

"So, what did you decide to do?" the senator asked. "Could you call for help?"

"No, my cell phone had fallen out of my pocket. I should have called before I started climbing but there is hardly any reception down there anyway. I sure would have tried if there had been. I gave out a few yells but I knew there was no one around for miles. So I just hung there, and my thoughts raced."

"A lot went through my mind - Jamie, Clara, and Ella mostly, and the farm. I considered that the hanging upside down would kill me, if the cat didn't. I knew I had to survive. I had to figure this out. Studying my options, I was left with few. I had to get my leg out of the trap. Then I remembered my pocket tool was still with me. It had always been a good friend in times of need."

"And then it came to me - just how serious this really was. I had heard about the past owner of our farm losing his leg from gangrene, after working too hard trying to keep the wolves from the door. It was then that I knew what I had to do. The leg was going to have to go, if I was going to get out of there. I'd take my chances with the cat when I got to the bottom. I did have my knife. I started chuckling to myself, thinking how crazy life can get, as I began working myself up for what I had to do."

"Taking my belt off somehow, I slipped it around my thigh. This took a while, as I had to rest in between efforts, falling back when I tired out. I got it real tight and tied it off. I'd read about others having to cut off a limb to escape an accident but never thought it would be me. I flipped open the knife blade. I laughed about the fact that I had sharpened it the other day but stopped when I recalled how well the saw worked on the branch that day too. I started cutting through my jeans well above the knee. I could see the bone sticking out below it but tried to avoid looking at it."

"You were willing to cut your leg off to escape?" the senator said.

"Well, I wasn't about to be no Gus McCray"

The senator sat back in his chair.

"My timing wasn't very good, and when I started making the first cut, I think I passed out again. When I came to, my arms were hanging down and being clawed at. I quickly pulled them up, and then realized my knife was gone. *Damn it, I lost another one.*

It was just like me to drop something when it's important - like that fly ball missed catch in the last inning at the school game. Funny the things you think about, at times like these."

"Not much light was left. It got dark, and I could see the moon rising. Everything was literally upside down from my view, hanging there. It was vivid through the pain. Somehow it makes you sharper. Then it puts you out, when it becomes overwhelming. The cat was always there. At that point, in my loneliness and despair, I guess she was as much my friend, as my enemy. It seemed she was all that I had left; my grim reaper, my death."

"They say, on the battlefield, the last thing men do, is cry out for their mothers. Well, I cried out as loud and long as I could for my best friend, greatest defender, and closest companion on the farm. That was my dog, Ace. That's the last I remember, until waking up on the hospital helicopter pad."

"There I heard the EMT tell the doctors that "there was no pulse", and he was sure I was dead, before they took off from the canyon. He said the people there had tried to save me, and got me free from the rock and the mountain lion, but that it was too late. He told them that the dog had jumped in the rescue basket with me, at the last moment, so they just kept flying to the hospital, not wanting to risk another landing."

* * * * *

My boss had mentioned my name, and I heard it through the massive wooden door. Since I was now considered a rescue dog, and carried the designated harness, I was allowed to be there that day with Evan, though they wouldn't let me in, and I had to wait outside with another "security guard". But when I heard Evan call for me, I just couldn't stand it. So, I started scratching and clawing at the bottom of the door, even though the person kept telling me to stop, and pulling back on my leash.

When someone opened the door from the other side to see what was going on, I charged in, pulling the tether from the holder. There was Evan, sitting near the front of the room, facing a row of chairs and faces looking right at him. Now they were looking at me, as I rushed down the aisle and got to Evan's side. I quickly saw he was okay, then sat at attention next to him.

"Ace! You shouldn't have come in here! I guess I did call your name though, which was my mistake. Well, there you go senators; this is Ace. In my estimation, he is the greatest farm dog there ever was."

He finished off by saying, "My coming back around reminds me of a time on the farm when we had an electrician out to fix a problem that I just couldn't solve, no matter how hard I tried. He arrived, and when he went to check it, the thing worked, and it has ever since. I stood back in amazement. He stood back too. He paused, and told me about what a wise old person told him once: 'There are just some things in life you're never going to figure out.'"

Well I know what happened up there in the sky that night. My short tail swept the marble floor.

The senator looked at me, then leaned back in his chair and said, "Thank you for being here, and for your testimony. I think we've all been humbled a little today."

"And thank you, sir, for allowing me the opportunity to speak to this fine institution."

The farm bill proposal passed through the committee the next day, with Evan and Jamie in the audience. It went to the full floor for consideration the following month. We watched on C-Span together, from the farm house, with me, Evan, Ella and Clara all there. I saw Evan watch some different numbers come up on the television screen.

"It passed!" he said, "With some compromises and changes but still pretty well intact. If the president now signs it, we have a new farm bill," and he hugged Ella.

I heard the commotion in the house a week later, and again scratched at the door. Clara let me in, and we were all at the television again. This time watching a man at a big desk with flags on both sides sign something.

"It's done, Ella," Evan said.

"They did the right thing, Evan."

Sensing the excitement in the room, I ran a few circles around them all on the living room floor, then sat at attention, hoping for a pet.

"Good job, Ace," Clara said.

Prices for corn, soybeans, and wheat rose the next spring. Livestock prices followed upwards the next fall. Farmers could sell more of their corn profitably, and cattle feeders cut back a little on how much they fed them, reducing the oversupply of beef to the market.

Farmers stored some of the extra crop in a government program that kept it off the market when prices were too low. The reserve of grain was to be used if a sudden drought or other disaster might hit.

Evan told Jamie, one day on the phone, that he thought consumers were happier since they worried about food supply and the risk of climate change disrupting production. It was the last thing they needed when they too were dealing with floods or the large forest fires that were hitting the west coast. It did raise food prices a little but not much, since most of the cost of food is in the processing, distribution, and marketing. There was plenty of grumbling by the buyers though. Evan said he guessed they had worries too.

He told Clara that regulators said that managing production, and using more conservation practices on the farm, would reduce carbon in the atmosphere. I think Evan and his neighbors are using those practices, and following the guidelines of the farm bill already.

I watched Evan walk a bit more confidently. I think he thought there was a lot of hope behind him, as a recognized spokesperson for one of the farming groups. Things relaxed on the farm some. When I went to town in the back of a newer pickup, the main street was busy. There was a sense of confidence on people's faces. And some were faces I hadn't even seen before. They said the population of the town was up. I stayed in the back of the pickup, while Clara and my boss went in the grocery store.

"How's your boss?" the passerby said, as she stroked my head.

I closed my eyes just partly, as the feeling of her hand was good, and thought, *He's more than fine, and so is the farm. I know I'm here forever now, and so is this great place on earth.*

The Wind at My Nose

The sky is usually blue above me. On the ride home that day, though, it was especially blue. But I have days that seem like it just isn't. I still remember when Rosy died. That day the sky seemed gray, in my mind. Yet when I think of it, I'm pretty sure the sky was really blue that afternoon. I have to wonder how much she had to do with saving Evan's life.

We went by the place where the three hundred cows had chased me. Then we cruised by the old dirt road along the pasture and creek where I was ambushed by that nasty raccoon. The wind was in my nose again. I could smell and sense everything all at once. The wind was making my eyes water real bad, I think, since tears kept blowing away in the breeze. I rubbed my face on Bean's fur, as she rode close beside me in the bed of the truck. Both our noses were pointed forward out the same side.

The sky was sure blue that day.

The farm? Yes, it's still going strong, just like me. This time it's lasted in the same owners' hands for thirty-five years now. That's longer than it ever has. I think my boss is sure out of the woods with it now. That's good, because I want to live here forever. Maybe I will, in some form or another. I want him to bury me alongside all the other dogs that have lived here.

I guess we're all just passing through, while the farm passes on to families that follow.

There have been many attempts to mess up the farm program again. The buyers always want it cheaper than we can raise it. And prices drop from time to time. Sure, they've got pressures too but they need to keep fairness in mind. The weather is still making it risky, and getting worse with climate change. My boss says, "Eternal vigilance is the only way." I guess he learned that from me, and now Beans, as we sit on the front porch looking out for varmints. She always jumps first now, and I let her.

Over time, and in my later years now, I've figured out that maybe I'm not the greatest farm dog. It really doesn't matter if I am or not. Though I sure do love this farm, and give it my all - more than another other dog, I'll argue. But this has to be the best farm ever. Yet I know it is only one in a sea of farms, just like the stars above.

May they all prosper and thrive, for the next dogs to take my place.

I'm not sure who that one will be here.

But I heard the name "Millie" in the wind last night.

Epilogue

I've come to realize that all the critters I chased around really aren't that bad. They're just like you and me, trying to get by and make a living. A few, when they get too big, are a bit piggish and need to be pushed away from the trough. The heifers—well, they were just having a little fun with me. That's okay, as long as they don't take it too far. All of them have different interests than me, but that doesn't make them bad.

Maybe we all have to share a little bit more and know that we each have our place and our job. Forget about ourselves some. Rodents clean up scraps. Cats eat rodents for food. And so on. I wonder if structuring our house in such a way that everyone can play their part, for the whole thing to go along better, is smart. Then I'm sure the farm and the cities can go on and on. It's about culture. Agriculture, and the way it was, really kept up with community. *It was community.* Keep that word in mind as we move forward, as I think there will always be a place for the farm and for dogs like me.

And another thing. Our earth; I saw it good while flying over. So beautiful, yet I hear it's so hurting, and maybe even some parts dying. I think we just need to nurse it more. To lick its wounds until they go away. I know we can heal it, if we just try hard enough. You know, it is our master. I saw the city and country all at once too. The city saved my boss, and the farm is what reared me. I got to respect them both and it's sure clear we can work together.

Dogs love to howl and bark at night. I'm sure not an exception, having got my fair share of scolding late in the evening, while my nose was to the heavens. Do you realize how many stars are really out there? They sure have been there long before us. Since that's the case, they've seen everything that happened down here on this little earth; the good and the bad.

Most think that the dogs are just talking to neighbor dogs when they bark, since we usually get into trouble when we visit them. So we talk across the sound waves. That's sure true. Did you know every sound wave goes on forever? I guess it's kind of like that ripple in a still pond when I take a step into it. It travels right across the whole area, it seems. And then comes back to me if I wait long enough.

There's always been a reason for howling. Certainly there's been an instinctual desire to do it. But, what if those sound waves I made with my little mouth and short nose kept going on past the earth's atmosphere and carried clear out into the stars beyond? Crazy, huh? I think about Jessie calling out to his horses when picking corn, or Homer talking to Harriet over supper. Where did the sound go but into the heavens? So that sound is still out there? Vibrations and reverberations coming back, maybe after bouncing off a star that's light-years away?

My same howls, though later than the previous utterances from Jessie and Homer, came from the same place. I suppose maybe they bounced of the same star or planet and are chasing them back. You know how much I like chasing. Even more than that, I like catching. And on those starlight, moonlight nights, my mouth was open, along with my ears.

Maybe, just maybe, that's how I know. The whole story was right there in the heavens, for me to simply catch.

I'm good at that.